Peaches on Top

Peaches Monroe's Diary

BOOK #4

ANGIE PEPPER

Chapter 1

Sunday, January 1st

I woke up to the sound of a butler clearing his throat politely.

The world was upside-down. No. Not the whole world. Just your girl, Peaches.

I was face-down on a sofa that smelled better than you'd expect a sofa to smell. Memories came rushing back. I was on a nice-smelling sofa, inside a Malibu mansion, after having driven all night to profess my feelings for a certain handsome actor. The reunion with Dalton Deangelo had gone well enough, and then... when we should have been enjoying our Happily Ever After, there was nothing.

The last thing I remembered was asking to use the washroom so I could freshen up after my all-night drive. I'd cleaned myself up in the gleaming marble bathroom, then stopped to rest on a nearby sofa to catch up with my thoughts. The sofa had been soft and inviting. I'd been overwhelmed by a powerful urge to be horizontal, just to rest my eyes a minute, and then sleep must have taken me.

The butler cleared his throat again.

My head swam as I propped myself up to a seated position. "How long was I out? What day is it?"

Dalton's butler, Bernard, replied in his British accent, "You've been asleep for three and a half hours, Ms. Monroe. It's two o'clock in the afternoon, but it is still New Year's Day."

"Two o'clock," I said, rubbing my eyes. "Does that mean I missed out on that lavish New Year's Day brunch you promised me... about four hours ago?"

The middle-aged man gave me a warm-hearted smile. "You haven't missed anything. I was preparing brunch when I heard your snores, so I held off on putting the french toast on the grill."

"You must have heard someone else's snores," I said with indignation. "I don't snore."

Bernard pressed his lips together tightly and said nothing.

"My dad, on the other hand, definitely snores," I said. "He's got red chest hair, and my mom calls him her snoring baboon, but I didn't inherit the snoring genes. Or the red chest hair."

Bernard nodded. "I see. In any case, I closed the door to this guest room so that your slumber wouldn't be disturbed by the sounds of *anyone else* in the vicinity snoring."

"You're the best." I stood up, flicked my blond hair over my shoulders, and looked around. "Where's the kitchen? I'd murder someone for a coffee right now. If you brew me a pot, I'll help you get brunch ready."

"Right this way," Bernard said.

I followed him down a generously wide hallway and into a kitchen that was bigger than the commercial kitchens of the restaurants back on Baker Street.

Bernard pulled an apron over his clothes. He didn't wear the stereotypical tuxedo worn by butlers in black-and-white movies. He wore crisp gray trousers and a white button-down shirt.

He handed me an apron. I pulled it on over my sequin-covered silver party dress, which I'd been wearing so long that I feared it might not peel off again.

Bernard frowned at me. "If you'd like to change into something more comfortable, I'm sure I could find something around here."

"I doubt that," I said. "You and your boss both have skinny hips, whereas I am internationally famous for my curves." I waved a hand. "This disco ball dress is surprisingly comfortable. Plus I didn't make it to my New Year's Eve party last night, so now's my only chance to wear it until—"

Dalton entered the kitchen and finished my sentence. "Until you take it off." He fixed me with his emerald-green eyes.

I felt the heat rising in my body and my cheeks flushing.

Bernard cleared his throat again. He was very good at that. He began pouring me a cup of coffee.

Dalton waved at the enormous spread on the kitchen island and asked his butler, "What's going on here? Where did all this food come from?" He looked genuinely shocked by the sight.

I waved at the croissants. "These are called carb-o-hy-drates," I said slowly. "Try one. You'll love it."

Dalton stepped back as though the calories from the carbohydrates might fly through the air and cause body fat.

"I never eat on New Year's Day," he said. "That's when I begin my three-day cleansing fast."

"No way," I said. "I've never heard of anything so crazy." I turned to the butler for backup.

Bernard gave me a tired look. "It's true," he said. "Mr. Deangelo begins every year with a multi-day water fast. By January third, I'm usually calling various headhunters to see about a change in employment."

"That's not true," Dalton said, glowering.

Bernard turned away without another word. He busied himself chopping strawberries.

Dalton said to me, "Fine. I may get a *wee bit* grumpy toward the end of the three days."

Bernard made a choking sound.

Dalton said, "This year will be easier." He gave me a dazzling smile. "Because you'll be here to keep my mind off eating."

"Maybe I'll join you in your three-day cleansing fast or whatever," I said. "Nisha and her boyfriend Noah are always talking about how fasting makes your mind clear. You know what? I'm already feeling refreshed. This fasting thing is easy."

Dalton pointed to my face. "You're literally eating a croissant right now."

"Am I?" I batted my eyelashes, playing dumb. "But it's so light and fluffy. Croissants shouldn't count. They're mostly air."

Dalton licked his lips. "That light-and-fluffy, mostly-air croissant does look good."

I finished my croissant, grabbed another one, and brought it toward him. "Try it," I said.

He pressed his lips together and backed up. "Nope," he said. "I'm already fourteen hours in."

"Come to the dark side," I said, moving in on him like a villain. "We have cookies."

I brought the croissant up and pressed it against his closed mouth. Flakes stuck to his dark upper-lip stubble.

He inhaled audibly, whimpered, then smacked the pastry out of my hand. Flakes sprayed our faces. The croissant landed on the floor, sending more flakes flying.

I put my hands on my hips. "You're wasting perfectly good food. What am I going to do with you?"

Bernard said, "There's no use in trying to convince him to eat, Ms. Monroe. It's going to be a bumpy three days, but at least we have each other."

I turned to the butler. "Is this what you meant when you said I got here just in time?"

"Yes," he replied.

I turned back toward Dalton, but he was gone. There was no sign of him. I yelled down the hallway. "Dalton? Where'd you go? I'll play hide-and-seek with you, but I need a coffee first or I'll just fall asleep again!"

There was no response.

"He's probably on the treadmill," Bernard said. "He likes to exercise to keep his energy up during the beginning of the fast. Exercise also prevents muscle loss, so that he only burns fat."

"Is he serious about fasting for three days?"

Bernard nodded and beckoned for me to come closer. Whispering, he said, "He has to. You didn't hear it from me, but Mr. Deangelo gained seven pounds over Christmas."

I snorted. "He's practically enormous now," I said.

"He's contractually obligated to lose it before he resumes filming on *One Vamp to Love*."

"That sucks. How'd he manage to gain seven pounds? Was it you, Bernard? Did you slip him carbs?"

Bernard looked down at the fruit salad he was making. "I'm afraid he let his guard down last month while spending time with... another friend."

"You mean Harper," I said. "The *other* curvy blonde. My butt double. Interesting. Harper made him gain weight, and now I bet he's afraid I'll do the same." I rubbed my chin thoughtfully. "I suppose that smashing a croissant into his face was not the reassurance he was looking for."

"I was surprised he smelled it," Bernard said. "You may have nearly broken him."

"I wouldn't want that. I swear I was only joking. I'd never sabotage his career."

"Of course not," Bernard said.

"Speaking of Harper, what's going on with those two? Is he really going to break up with her immediately, just because I showed up on his doorstep with my speech?"

"They already parted ways," Bernard said. "Something must have happened at the Dragonfly Resort. When they returned, the poor girl was heartbroken."

"Good," I said.

Bernard raised an eyebrow.

I quickly added, "I mean, it's not good that she's heartbroken, since she's actually a sweet girl, but it's good that..." I had no idea how to finish the sentence. I was glad that Harper was out of the picture. I had Dalton all to myself, and we could... what? Live happily ever after? With me eating croissants and him fleeing the scene? I picked up my coffee and took a sip.

Bernard said nothing, but he did give me a look that said he understood my complicated feelings about Harper's broken heart, and that it was okay.

After I'd finished my coffee, I searched around for a broom and cleaned up the mess I'd made on the floor.

Then Bernard and I pulled two chairs up to the kitchen island and settled in to enjoy our New Year's Day brunch.

The butler held his flute of mimosa up to toast my glass. "To the first of many new years. Forgive me for gushing, but it is my absolute pleasure to be spending the first meal on the first day of the year with you, Ms. Monroe."

"Call me Peaches," I said.

"Not yet," he said. Smiling, he clinked his glass to mine.

Chapter 2

An hour after our mimosas, Bernard was tidying up, and I was still grazing on the brunch spread when my phone rang. It was my best friend and roommate.

As I dug my phone out of my purse, the butler dried his hands on a dish towel and murmured that he would give me some privacy.

"Hey, girl," I said cheerfully.

Nisha replied in her usual British accent, which was less posh than Bernard's. "Where the bloody hell do you think you are?"

"I'm in Malibu," I said.

"Shut up. Where are you, really?"

"I drove all night. I'm in California, at Dalton's house."

The other end of the call was silent.

"Hello? Nisha? Are you still there?"

"Hang on," she whispered. I heard a door closing. "Okay. I'm in my bedroom now, where the guys can't hear me. Does Adrian know where you are?"

"I haven't told him," I said. "I sent him a bunch of text messages from the road, but he hasn't gotten back to me. Would you do me a huge favor and, um, break up with him for me?"

She snorted. "Peaches!"

"It was worth a shot," I said with a sigh.

"What's happening? Are you back with Dalton?"

"I don't know. Nothing's official, but he hasn't kicked me out of his house yet, even though I did crush my croissant on his beautiful face."

She groaned. "Peaches, I'm too hungover to hear about your sexual exploits. You crushed your croissant on his beautiful face? What does that even mean? Never mind! I don't want to know."

"Ha ha," I said, and explained about the carbohydrates. Then I said, "Tell Noah I'm sorry I stole his car, but I had to get out of there before Adrian proposed."

Nisha giggled. "You were wrong about that," she said. "Adrian wasn't going to propose to you last night."

"What?"

She repeated herself. "He had no intention of proposing to you."

I gasped. "He didn't? I can't believe him! How dare he act like he was going to propose, with his hints, and a ring, and everything, and then not do it? What a jerk!"

In the silence that followed, I imagined Nisha rolling her eyes at me.

She said, "Ask me what happened at the party."

"What happened at the party?"

"There was a proposal," she said, stifling a giggle. "A ring and a proposal."

"Are you still drunk?"

She giggled again. "Maybe a little."

"What happened?"

She gushed, "Noah proposed to me. Can you believe it? The whole thing with Adrian proposing was just a smoke show, to keep me off the scent so Noah could surprise me. Oh, Peaches, I wish you'd been there. It was perfect. Just perfect."

I should have congratulated her immediately, but I was struggling to grasp the concept that I'd stolen Noah's car and run away for nothing.

"Adrian didn't want to marry me?" My voice cracked. "But he promised me a surprise."

"There *was* a surprise for you," Nisha said patiently, because my best friend was basically a saint. She explained, "Adrian's been saving up his earnings from all his jobs, and he was going to take you on a nice vacation. Somewhere warm and tropical."

"Oh," I said flatly.

Nisha cleared her throat, reminding me of Bernard.

I finally remembered my manners.

"Congratulations on your engagement," I said. "Wow. What a surprise. You and Noah. Talk about a big turnaround. You were pining over him for years, then you had lousy sex, and now you're getting married."

"The sex is much better now," she said.

"I should hope so," I said. "Are you crushing your croissant in his beautiful face?"

"Regularly," she said.

"That's my girl."

"How long are you staying down there? We need to start planning the wedding. Noah wants to release doves. There's a lady who rents them out for special events. She's also got alpacas. Or is it llamas? I always mix them up. I think it's alpacas. Anyway, when you rent the doves, she throws in the alpaca. People like getting their pictures taken with the alpaca, just as a side thing. Don't worry. It's not like I'm making it an entirely alpaca-themed wedding, although... they're native to Peru, right? I could have Peruvian food. Oh, but what if my family is offended? I'd better not. The aunties wouldn't like that. It's bad enough I'm marrying the whitest of white boys." Nisha's ancestors were from India. She let out a long squeal. "I'm getting married! To Noah!"

"I wish I could be there to congratulate you in person," I said.

"You don't have to lie," she said. "And besides, I knew this was coming. Ever since you met Dalton Deangelo, when you fell into his arms from a ladder, I knew he had your heart. It was inevitable that this day would come. But it's okay. I have Noah. You can abandon me. I won't perish without you."

"Stop being stoic," I said. "I can hear your chin lifting and your upper lip stiffening."

"My chin is lifted. My upper lip is stiff."

"Stop it right now. Your stoicism is breaking my heart."

"Then have your Hollywood fling, get it all out of your system, then get your butt back here with Noah's car."

I didn't say anything. It had been a long drive, and I wasn't relishing the idea of doing it in reverse.

After a moment, Nisha asked, "What day are you coming back? Wednesday? Is three days in Hollywood enough for you?"

Rather than answer her question, I asked, "What would Noah want for his car? It's a sturdy vehicle, and I've got some money. Tell him I'll give him ten percent over book value."

"Peaches!"

"Fine. Twenty percent."

"You have to come back here. What about Adrian?"

"What about Adrian?" I said mockingly. "I'm mad at Adrian. I thought he was going to propose to me. It wasn't fair of him to string me along like that. Sure, it was a cool idea to trick you so Noah could surprise you, but Adrian should have let me in on the secret."

"Let me get this straight. You ditched me at the party last night, stole Noah's car, drove to California to be with another man, and now you're mad at Adrian?"

"Yes."

"I'm... just... I mean... wow. This is *a lot*. Even for you, Peaches."

"It is?"

"Adrian's going to be crushed when he finds out you slept with Dalton."

"Oh, but I haven't slept with Dalton," I said excitedly. "I would never do that without officially breaking up with Adrian. I may not be perfect, but I do have some standards."

"Right. You steal cars, but you do draw the line at cheating on your boyfriend."

The way she was painting the picture did not make for a flattering image of little ol' me.

"It all seemed so wild and romantic last night," I said wearily. "But I have to admit, if I weren't me, and I heard about what I did, I don't think I'd like myself."

There was a long silence.

"Nisha?"

"Sorry," she replied. "Were you still talking? I couldn't hear you over my new diamond engagement ring."

"I wish I could see it," I said.

"I hear something in your voice," she said. "You're not planning to come home anytime soon, are you?"

"Not for a while, no. Can you talk to Noah about the car?"

"Borrow it as long as you need. He doesn't use it, anyway."

"Thanks. Is Adrian there? Is that why you had to go to your bedroom to talk to me?"

"Yes. He came over last night after the party to celebrate the engagement. We thought you'd be here. He slept over in your bed. He told us he hoped you'd come back from your parents' house so he could wake up with you in the morning."

"He—" I couldn't finish the question. My throat closed up. I had been surprised by the mental image of Adrian sleeping in my bed, waiting for me to come home so he could wake up with me.

I felt something. Something bad, like guilt. I'd hurt him. He'd hurt me first, by not proposing, but what I'd done to him was worse. Adrian could talk tough at times, but underneath it all, he was as sensitive as anyone. He was the guy who'd adopted an injured rat and paid for its vet bills.

Nisha asked, "Do you want me to get Adrian on the line for you? My phone's charged up. You can talk to him on here if you want."

"I guess we should do that. Pull the Band-Aid off quickly. It's not going to get any easier if I drag it out. Sure."

"Hang on," she said.

There was the sound of the door opening.

I heard the murmur of Noah and Adrian talking in the kitchen, sounding serious, then going quiet.

"Take my phone," Nisha said, presumably to Adrian. "It's Peaches."

Adrian replied, "Why would I want to talk to her on the phone?"

"Because," Nisha said. "It's important. She's got something to tell you."

There was a silence. I wished I could see Adrian's face so I'd know what he was up to. Was he joking around, or did he already know why I was phoning? My stomach twisted. The party dress I'd worn all night suddenly became intolerably itchy.

"No thanks," Adrian said, speaking loudly enough to be clear as a bell even without the phone held up to his mouth. "If *your* best friend has anything to say to me, anything at all, she can do it in person."

"Just take the phone," Nisha said. "Why are you being so difficult?"

"Nisha," said the other guy in the room, Noah. He spoke gently but firmly. "My parents had a security tracker installed on that car. I looked it up as soon as Peaches called you. We know she's in California. Adrian knows exactly where she is."

There was another silence.

Then Adrian said, "I've got stuff to do today. Tell Peaches I'll talk to her when she comes to her senses and comes back to town."

Nisha pleaded with him to just take the phone and talk to me. I heard the back door slam.

Noah said to Nisha, "Adrian's really upset. And now I feel anxious. He's my best friend, besides you, and he's really hurting right now."

She replied, "Why are you looking at me like that? I didn't do anything to Adrian."

He said, "You need to talk some sense into your friend."

"There's no talking to Peaches when she gets an idea in her head," Nisha said. "You know how she is."

"I do know," Noah said. "We all have our blind spots. I hope you can help her open her eyes the way you helped me. That girl needs to know the world doesn't revolve around her and her alone."

Whispering, Nisha said, "She's still on the phone. She can hear everything."

"Good," Noah said, louder. "Peaches, I think you're one of the most interesting, fun girls I've ever met, but you're making a huge mistake turning your back on Adrian. He'd move mountains for you."

"She's made up her mind," Nisha said.

"We'll see," Noah said.

I heard Nisha breathing into the phone, then a door closed again. "I'm back in my room again. Are you still there?"

"Yes," I said. "I heard everything."

"Sorry about that. You know how guys can be. They're so loyal to each other, and Noah has really taken to Adrian. What he said about you making a big mistake, it was just his opinion."

"What about you? Do you think I'm making a mistake?"

There was a pause, then she said, "You and Adrian sure do fight a lot. Are you like that with Dalton?"

"How should I know? We've barely had any time together as a couple."

"Then it's a good thing you're there now. You can find out," she said. I heard the squeak of her bedsprings as she got more comfortable. "Now, tell me everything. What time did you get there? What did Dalton say when he saw you? What does his house look like?"

I switched the phone to my cool ear, poured another coffee, and gave my best friend the information she wanted. I giggled and played up all the fun aspects, but beneath the surface, I wasn't so fun and giggly. I kept thinking about Adrian, our unfinished business, and Noah's suggestion that Adrian would move mountains for me.

Did Noah see something I didn't?

Chapter 3

After my phone call with Nisha, I sat in Dalton's enormous kitchen alone with my thoughts. Staring out the window at the blue, cloudless sky was calming, but I still had one big problem.

What now? My first attempt to officially break up with Adrian had failed. If he wouldn't talk to me on the phone, what else could I do? Were there lawyers who could draw up papers? The idea of Adrian being "served" breakup papers made me snort.

I looked down at my phone and composed a short message: I, Peaches Monroe, officially break up with you, Adrian Stromquist, effective immediately.

I sent the message.

It immediately bounced back to me with the message: This number is no longer in service.

I swore at my phone. I was angry at Adrian, but I also had to admire his commitment to the mind game.

I put the phone away, looked out the window again, and tried to focus on the here and now.

From where I sat, I had a perfect view of the pool in the backyard. It was shimmering in an extremely photogenic way. It looked so inviting. Here it was, the first day of January, and a dip in the pool looked perfect. The weather wasn't hot, but it was downright balmy for January. Back home, people were wearing winter jackets.

My mind eventually cleared of its anxieties and settled on where I was.

New questions came to mind. For example, if Dalton never ate, why did he have such a big kitchen? Was it because he threw parties for fancy Hollywood people? Did he have a group of friends who came over regularly to play video games and raid his fridge, like I did? What did he do in his free time?

I had no idea. I'd never seen him on his home turf.

As I was gazing out the window, two shirtless men appeared poolside—Dalton and another guy. The other guy was in his forties, with bright-red hair on his head, a clean waxed chest, and multiple tattoos all over both arms. He stood watching as Dalton did pushups at the edge of the pool.

Behind me, Bernard cleared his throat to politely let me know he'd re-entered the kitchen.

Without looking back, I asked the butler, "Is that red-haired guy a buddy or a personal trainer?"

"He's one of the personal trainers," Bernard said. "Mr. Deangelo has two on rotation."

"Is that normal?"

"For an actor, yes. Have you thought about what you'd like for dinner?"

"Easy now. Give me a few hours to digest that brunch we just ate, big guy!"

Bernard chuckled at my response and muttered about pulling out some recipe books.

I watched Dalton sweating in the sun. He was working hard on the pushups. I heard the sound of recipe books being flipped through.

I asked Bernard, "Do you think I should go out there and try a few pushups out of solidarity? When in California, do as the Californians do?"

"I wouldn't advise that. I tried to join in a few years back and discovered aches and pains in muscles I didn't know I had. However, if you're interested in doing something at your own pace, there is a full gym down on the lower level that you can use at your leisure."

"There's another level below here?"

"Yes," he said brightly. "I suppose you haven't seen everything yet. I do apologize for not giving you a full tour. Would you like one now?"

"Sure," I said.

Bernard set aside the recipe books, and we began the tour.

The house had seven bedrooms, each with its own washroom, and countless other rooms, many of them unused.

"This is the box room," Bernard said. We stood in the doorway of a room containing nothing but the cardboard boxes from various appliances and electronics.

"But why?" I asked. "Is your boss thinking about returning two hundred things before the warranty is up?"

Bernard furrowed his brow. "That's a good question. I don't know why we maintain a box room, but it seems to make Mr. Deangelo happy."

"And that's your job," I said. "Making Mr. Deangelo happy."

Without hesitation, Bernard replied, "My job is to keep him fed, clothed, and at his appointments on time. I believe happiness falls under your job description."

I let out a nervous laugh. "No pressure," I said. "The guy has absolutely everything, but I'm supposed to make him happy?"

"He doesn't have *everything*," Bernard said. "Not yet, anyway." He beckoned for me to come with him. "I'll show you the steam room."

The butler took me to a tiled room that reminded me of a place I'd once enjoyed with Adrian. The memory of our entangled bodies came back in such vivid detail that it took my breath away. The room began to spin. I leaned forward and placed my hands on a wooden bench for support. That, unfortunately, only brought back more sense memories. What was I doing? Had I lost my mind?

Bernard asked, "Is something wrong? You look upset. It's my fault for overwhelming you with the tour. I don't need to show you every inch of this place. I can let you explore on your own."

"It's not you, or the house," I said. "I came here in a rush, without thinking."

He didn't say anything, but he did give me the facial expression of a good listener, so I went on.

"It felt so wild and romantic at the time, last night, but it was actually pretty stupid and selfish. Oh, Bernard. What have I done?" I took a seat on the wooden bench. "When I came here, I left my boyfriend behind. I thought he was going to propose, but it turns out he wasn't."

I paused long enough for Bernard to say, "Good heavens."

"I know, right? I tried to set things right and officially break up with him today, over the phone, but he wouldn't let me."

"Breakups are never easy," Bernard said.

I stared at the butler's face, which was warm and friendly yet also professional. Looking at him made me feel less dizzy, less out of control. It was like having my dad around, but minus the weight of him knowing all of my personal history.

Bernard went on to say, "I am sorry to hear that you are having a difficult time. Is there any way that I can help?"

"Thanks for listening," I said.

He nodded.

"As for what else, I'll need my own room here," I said. "At least for tonight. I can't be in Dalton's room. Not until after I've broken up with Adrian."

Bernard didn't even blink. "Certainly. I did not want to make any assumptions, so I have already prepared a guest suite for you. It's the same room you used earlier, when you had your nap."

"Perfect," I said. "Can you do me another favor? When bedtime comes around, can you make sure I'm in there, and that there's a triple padlock on the door?"

He gave me a concerned look. "Mr. Deangelo would *never* break into your room, Ms. Monroe."

"The locks aren't for keeping him out. It's for keeping me in. Put the padlocks on the outside and secure me for the night."

He blinked. "I couldn't do that."

"Good, because I was just joking. Unless, of course, you have padlocks."

"I may have something in the garden shed..."

"Never mind. Forget I mentioned anything." I reached out a hand and let him help me up from my seat on the wooden bench. I was feeling a little better, but I still wanted to get out of the steam room. I kept seeing Adrian out of the corner of my eye.

As we walked out of the room, Bernard said, "This certainly has been an interesting new year so far. I can't wait to see what's in store for all of us."

"Me, neither. Can you give me the instructions for how to get back to my room? I need to make some more phone calls. My soon-to-be-ex-boyfriend has changed his number, but there's other business I can do."

He smiled. "This way." He checked the time on his phone as we walked. "By the way, some items will be here for you in about an hour. I hope you don't mind that I guessed at your dress size."

"Why did you have to guess? You could have measured me up with a tape when I was napping."

He gave me a horrified look. "I would never!"

I smiled, enjoying his horror.

He cleared his throat. "In any case, I have ordered a range of clothing options that should cover most activities, including swimming. You should have enough for a new outfit every day for the next month."

I stared at him in amazement. "And then what? Do I get kicked out of here after four weeks?"

"Yes," he said, his lips tight. "That is the house policy for guests who are not paying rent. Ha ha. Just kidding."

"You had me going for a minute," I said.

"What can I say? You bring out my lighter side, Ms. Monroe."

We reached the suite where I'd taken a nap earlier that day.

I had to ask Bernard if he'd also been joking about ordering me a month's worth of clothes. It did seem too good to be true. He assured me that he never joked about matters as serious as wardrobes. He'd also ordered a full complement of makeup and toiletries, all through a colleague of his who was a professional personal shopper.

With all of that settled, the butler left me to my private guest room and my phone calls.

I tried Adrian once more with a voice call, and got the notice of disconnection.

I tried his parents' house and got voicemail. I left a message asking him to call me, even though I knew he wouldn't.

I called my mother and checked in. She expressed her concerns about what I was up to, as expected, but she had her hands full with Elliot and couldn't talk for long.

Then I called Mr. Olivier and gave him the bad news that I was quitting, with zero days' notice.

"This is very unexpected," the seventy-something, French-accented man said. "I don't know what I'm going to do without you. Ooh! Perhaps I shall close the store and rent out the space to one of those fake butcher shops that sells patties made out of beans."

"Don't you dare," I said. "There's a perfect resume on top of your paperwork. The woman's name is Riley, and she can start tomorrow."

"Is she good?"

"She's not me, because who is, but I think she'll do."

My boss didn't sound convinced. "I'm actually at the store right now. I was picking up the deposit when you called." There was the sound of papers shuffling. "Let me see. Ah. Here's the resume. Riley. What sort of a name is that?" He sighed. "I suppose I'll have to interview her, but I'm not sure when I'll have the time. I have a flight back to Arizona later this week. I need to get out of this rainy weather."

"Give me Riley's phone number, and I'll call and make all the arrangements," I said. "I'm the one who left you high and dry, Mr. Olivier. Let me set things right."

He rattled off the woman's phone number without a moment's hesitation.

Chapter 4

It took a few hours, but I finished wrapping up my business back home, including hiring Riley to take over my job "on a temporary basis." She was more than willing to take on managing the bookstore permanently, but I wasn't ready to let it go. And why would I? I hadn't even been in LA for twenty-four hours. There was a good chance my life would flame out within a week. I might have to leave in my stolen car, humiliated, but at least I'd still have a job to go back to.

I set down the phone. There was an ache in my head. It wasn't a full-blown headache. Just the strain of my brain trying to figure out what the future might look like. My poor brain. It was only trying to do its job of predicting the days ahead, but it had so little solid data to go on.

There was a gentle knock on the door, and Bernard called out, "Ms. Monroe, your wardrobe has arrived."

I jumped up from the bed and flung open the door, expecting to find the butler holding a few shopping bags. What he actually had was a rolling cart, like the kind used on movie or photography sets. Back when I'd done my first underwear modeling stint the previous summer, I'd seen plenty of rolling carts. None of them had been as full as this one.

"This is too much," I said. "It must have cost a fortune. I can't possibly..." I looked at Bernard. He wasn't saying anything. I laughed and said, "Oh, who am I kidding? Of course I can. I'm only making a fuss so you won't think I'm spoiled, but what's wrong with being spoiled? And besides, it's not a car or a house. It's just clothes."

The man's expression remained neutral as he wheeled in the rack. Then he asked, "Would you *like* for me to arrange a car or a house for you, Ms. Monroe?"

"Pump the brakes, Bernard! It was just a joke!"

He gave me a faint smile.

I asked, "Where's Dalton?"

"I believe he's in the steam room. I can take you there if you don't remember the way."

I imagined visiting the steam room, and seeing Dalton's glistening body. Would he be tired from his workout and fasting? Probably not too tired to cause trouble. If I were to find myself in a steamy room with him, things would rapidly heat up in more ways than one. We'd recently shared a steamy moment together in a hot tub over Christmas, and it had been hot, indeed. Luckily for me, my father walked into the Dragonfly Lodge's pool room before things got out of control. Who knows what the security cameras might have caught on film.

As appealing as a steam room adventure was, I couldn't go. I'd promised myself—and Nisha—that nothing would happen with Dalton until I'd officially broken up with Adrian. However—and it was a pretty big however—who was to say I *hadn't* broken up with Adrian? He knew where I was and what I was up to. I'd gotten verbal confirmation from him when he'd yelled at Nisha's phone. Didn't that count? Would I be a bad person if I considered that official enough? I could forgive myself for breaking my word, but would Nisha ever let me forget it?

As I pondered ways to wriggle out of my verbal contract with Nisha, I grabbed a swimsuit from the rolling rack.

Bernard said, "It's a private steam room. You don't need swimwear."

"Oh," I said, quickly shutting down my waffling. "If the steam room is clothes-optional, then I'm definitely not going there."

"I understand," he said. "You can't go to the clothing-optional steam room with Mr. Deangelo because you haven't officially terminated your relationship with another party."

I shook my head. "I shouldn't have blabbed all my secrets to you. Is there such a thing as butler-guest confidentiality? You won't tell Dalton about my boyfriend back home, will you?"

"My loyalty is to Mr. Deangelo," Bernard said stiffly. "If he asks me directly, I must be honest." In a more relaxed tone, he added, "But if he doesn't ask directly, I don't see why I would bring it up."

"Thanks." I held the swimsuit against my body. It appeared to be the perfect size. "Great work on the clothes. I'll talk to your boss about getting you a raise."

"No need," he said lightly. "Mr. Deangelo is the best employer I've ever had."

"Does he pay you to say that? Blink twice if you're being held here against your will."

Bernard didn't blink.

"This is a gorgeous swimsuit," I said. "How private is the back yard? Can the neighbors see the pool area?"

He replied, "If they have binoculars, I suppose so."

"Then it's a good thing you got me a pretty swimsuit," I said. "I'm going to hit the pool and do a few laps. You can tell your boss where to find me."

"Very well." He nodded and left me to get changed.

I pulled on the azure swimsuit, tied my hair in a messy topknot, and headed toward the pool.

Dalton's house wasn't waterfront, but I could see the ocean from the highest point of the yard. The view could have been even more open, but an artful landscaper had placed blooming shrubs and trees around the property to give the pool area some privacy.

I took a few quick photos with my phone and sent them to Nisha.

Then I stepped into the pool.

The water was just cool enough to be refreshing.

I rolled my shoulders a few times, coaxing my body into relaxation, and began swimming.

The pool was large, for a private pool, but smaller than the community center pools I'd previously swam in. The number of laps I swam quickly added up, making me feel like an Olympic athlete.

Bernard came out to check that everything was to my liking.

"I'm in heaven," I told him.

He seemed pleased by that and left me to more swimming.

After I'd finished a personal-record-setting number of laps, I floated over to the corner and rested with my arms on the tiles, tilting my face up to the sun.

What a way to start a new year.

I congratulated myself on having made the right choice on New Year's Eve. Sure, a few people were upset with me, but once they came to visit, they'd understand. Not Adrian, of course. He'd hold it against me forever. He'd bring it up at every single family gathering, and he'd always be around, because of his connection to Elliot. I'd have to see Adrian forever, and he'd never let me forget the time I ditched him at a New Year's party and fled to Hollywood.

I began rehearsing a new speech in my head. The one I'd give Adrian when I finally got him on the phone. *Adrian, we gave it a solid try. You have to admit that it wasn't exactly working. We bickered like an old couple all the time. I'm okay with being a bickering old couple someday, but not now while we're young.*

He would then blame the bickering on me, saying that it took *two to tango*, so to speak, and that if I hadn't been so infuriating, ninety percent of our fights would never have happened.

Then I'd tell him *he* was the infuriating one, and I'd list off his character flaws, starting with his moody face.

I didn't know how long I'd been arguing with Adrian in my head when my thoughts were interrupted.

Dalton surprised me by doing a cannonball into the pool. My eyes had been closed, and when the water splashed over me, I screamed in surprise.

Dalton emerged from the water, laughing. He used his hands to push the water from his beautiful eyes and through his lush hair. Seeing him that way, wet and gleaming, framed by the California scenery, felt surreal, like I was watching a scene in a movie. His body looked even more muscular and chiseled than I remembered. Was this real, or was I in a computer simulation?

He swam toward me, his emerald-green eyes fixed on mine.

I floated up my foot and stopped him.

He tipped his face down and gently bit my toes.

I giggled and pulled my legs back toward me.

He swam forward and was suddenly against me. I was pinned in the corner of the pool. The heat of his almost-nude body radiated into me, in stark contrast to the chill of the water.

I put my palms on his chest to put some distance between us. My hands moved of their own accord, and I ran my fingers over his shoulders.

"You look really strong," I said. "I don't remember your muscles being this big when we were in the hot tub together, and that wasn't even a week ago. What is that personal trainer doing to you?"

He grinned. "Muscles always look bigger right after a workout. They get pumped up."

"Is that really true? The pump? I thought that was just something guys said to drive each other nuts, like how some girls say they only eat salads."

"It's real." He flexed his arms for me then kissed each bicep.

"Ew," I said.

His eyes danced with amusement. "Ew? I bet you won't be saying *ew* tonight, when these arms are holding me up so I can do all sorts of things to you." He swam closer again.

I quickly pinched my nose and sank underwater, ducking under his arm and getting away. "About that," I said when I'd resurfaced. "Would you mind if we, um, take things slow?"

He sank into the pool, his face low in the water, and moved toward me like a crocodile. "Don't you worry. I know just how to take it slow and make it last."

I squealed and moved backward, using the edge of the pool to propel myself toward the stairs.

"That's not what I meant," I said. "I think we should take it slow-slow. Bernard set me up in my own room, and I'd like to sleep there tonight. If it's all the same to you."

"It is not all the same to me."

"It's what I'd prefer."

Dalton shrugged his muscular, pumped shoulders. "I can take things slow... in any room of the house you want."

"You know what I mean," I said.

He stopped coming toward me and silently treaded water. "Did I do something wrong?" His brow furrowed with genuine-looking concern.

"Not at all," I said quickly. "It's just that..." I trailed off, finishing in my head with *I haven't broken up with the tall, blond guy whose name you always pretend you can't remember.*

Dalton raised an eyebrow. "Are you worried about messing up my three-day water fast?"

"Yes." I pointed a finger at him. "That's exactly what I'm worried about." *And definitely not about being a filthy two-timing cheater.*

"Fasting doesn't make me weak," he said. "After the first day, the body releases growth hormones. It's a survival instinct. I get sharper, and I have more energy to go after what I want. My dopamine levels shoot through the roof. When I'm on a three-day fast, nothing stands in my way. Whatever I want is mine."

I swallowed hard. "Challenge accepted."

He nodded.

"See you at dinner," I said, and quickly made my escape from the pool via the stairs. I could feel his gaze on my body.

He called after me, "I'm not eating dinner. Fasting, remember?"

I stopped in my tracks. It was hard for me to imagine a person not eating dinner. Skipping breakfast or lunch, sure, but dinner? I turned around slowly.

Dalton laughed. "Don't make that face," he said. "Of course I'll see you at dinner. I'll have some water and electrolytes, and you can enjoy Bernard's meal for both of us."

I put my hands on my hips. "Is this going to be weird? I'm totally comfortable with my figure, but will I develop some sort of complex if you're always sipping water while I'm eating? How often do you do this fasting thing?"

"Only at the start of a new year," he said.

I let out a sigh of relief.

He added, "Or the days before I have a shirtless scene at work."

I shook my head. "I've seen the show. You have shirtless scenes all the time."

He shrugged. "Then I'll have to find another way to burn off excess calories."

I held my hand to my chest. "Is that all I am to you?" I asked in mock outrage. "Two personal trainers aren't enough for you? You need me to be your third personal trainer?"

He answered with another shrug, which I actually found incredibly appealing. Everything he did was appealing.

I'd watched Dalton Deangelo on TV for years, as Sir Drake Cheshire. Hadn't I regularly fantasized about him—the actor or the character—I wasn't fussy—burning off calories with a certain curvy blonde? Of course I had.

Now my fantasy was about to come true. I already had a new wardrobe and a luxurious pool to swim in. In a few days, after I'd broken up with Adrian and Dalton had finished his fasting, I would get everything I'd ever wanted.

What could possibly go wrong?

Chapter 5

Monday, January 2nd

I woke up in my guest bedroom—alone, thank you very much—and enjoyed an amazing stretch. My body felt so good. Slightly sore from all the swimming, but in a good way. I'd slept for ten hours straight and felt completely rejuvenated. I was ready for my first full day in Malibu.

I took a long shower, sampling all the hair and body products the personal shopper had selected for me. Then I pulled on a thick white robe so I could take my time selecting my wardrobe for the day. Deep down, I knew I'd be pulling on the pair of pre-worn jeans and comfy T-shirt, but first I would entertain the idea of dressier outfits.

Nisha phoned when I was halfway through the rolling rack.

"Hi again," I said. "It feels like we've been talking more than we did when I lived there."

"There's more to discuss," she said.

"Should we talk about bridesmaid dresses? I'm assuming you want me to be your maid of honor."

"We can talk about that another time," Nisha said. "I'm just calling to let you know that Riley seems nice. I think she'll be a great fit for managing the bookstore. She was just here at the house, picking up the keys and security code. You got really lucky with her."

"It *was* pretty lucky she strolled into the store on December thirty-first. Talk about being in the right place at the right time."

"Peaches, you might not have a job here if and when you do come back. Adrian told me that Riley seems like an even better bookstore manager than you."

"Adrian said that? What? Why? Did he meet her this morning? Is he still hanging around at the house?"

"Um, yes. He's staying in your room. He says he misses you, and also that he's very depressed and can't be alone right now."

I snorted. "This is psychological warfare. He's trying to mess with my head. Kick him out of there. He doesn't pay rent, and I don't want him messing around with my stuff." I groaned. The idea of him sleeping in my bed while I wasn't there! I had to give the guy credit. His instincts for getting under my skin were well honed.

"You need to talk to him yourself," Nisha said.

"I called him eleventy-billion times, and his solution was to get his phone number disconnected. Before he did that, I even tried from Bernard's phone so he wouldn't know it was me. He still wouldn't pick up. Worst of all, now he's got Bernard's number. What if he calls him to start checking in on me, or making wild claims?"

"Wild claims such as... that he's still your boyfriend?"

"He's not my boyfriend," I said.

"That's not how he sees it. A bunch of us ordered pizza and played games here at the house last night, and even Sunshine and Brittany agreed with him that you two aren't officially over yet."

I let out an angry growl. "Whatever happened to the sisterhood? To girls sticking together?"

"You know those two," she said in a catty tone. "They're both madly devoted to the bloke, even though he's not interested in either of them."

"That gives me an idea," I said. "Adrian's got a strong psychological game, but he's still just a man. How about tonight, you invite the girls over. Later, when Adrian's in my bed, you put on some mood music, light some of your most sensual incense, and shove one or both of them into my room?"

She gasped. "Peaches!"

"All's fair in love and war. If those two won't do it, maybe I can hire someone. A professional. What's the going rate for seduction by the hour?"

She didn't answer.

The silence stretched out.

I sighed. Point taken. I asked, "How's your diamond ring looking this morning?"

"Dazzling," she said immediately. "I love how it catches the morning light when I'm at the sink. How did you know I was admiring it just now?"

"I'm psychic," I said. "If only I could use my powers for something besides knowing when you're staring at your engagement ring."

In a serious tone, she said, "I'm sorry Adrian wasn't going to propose to you on New Year's Eve. I'm sure if you came back, he would do the whole thing, down on one knee."

"No thanks. Is he there now? Sneak up to him and put your phone on his ear. I can give him a short version of my speech before he even knows what hit him."

"He's out jogging with Noah."

"I can wait. Come on, Nisha, you've got to do this for me. I need to... *you know*."

"I don't know. What are you getting at? Did you already cave last night and sleep with Dalton?" She sounded disappointed.

"Nope," I said proudly. "But you should have seen him in the pool. He was so yummy. Then he kept making me laugh all through dinner last night. He kept touching my feet with his feet under the table. We went for a walk after dinner, and we held hands the whole time."

"That sounds awfully romantic," she said. "In some ways, it sounds more intimate than if you'd just gone at it like wild rabbits."

"I know," I said wearily. "Am I a horrible two-timing cheater?"

There was a long pause, then she said, "You really need to talk to Adrian and set things right."

"That's what I'm trying to do. Will you help me ambush him when he gets back from his jog?"

"I'll try," she said.

We had some time to kill before the boys returned from their jog, so Nisha asked me to tell her more about Dalton, his butler, and the house.

I did, and we also chatted about her wedding plans. She was definitely set on getting the doves and the alpaca.

I heard the kitchen door open. Noah and Adrian had returned from their jog. They were giving each other a hard time over who was slower.

Next, there was a scuffle. When the line went quiet, which I took to mean the phone was on Adrian's ear, I launched into my speech.

"Adrian, I officially terminate our—"

I was cut off by the sounds of more scuffle.

In the distance, I heard Adrian yelling, "Not today, Satan!" Then he cursed out Nisha for trying to ambush him.

Suddenly his voice was in my ear, loud and clear, and he said, "We'll discuss this in person. Until then, I'm not speaking to you."

There were more sounds of the phone being handled, then Nisha was back. "That went better than

I expected," she said. "He's pretty strong for a skinny guy."

"Thanks for trying," I said.

"I should get going to work," she said. "I've got a full day of sampling wine ahead of me."

"Poor thing."

"What are you up to today?"

I took a seat on the edge of the bed and stared at the rolling rack of clothes. "Dalton promised he'd drive me around and show me some local sights."

"Lucky you," she said. "By the way, Noah said you can have the car for book value minus a friend discount of five percent."

"That guy's a keeper," I said. "Even with the man bun."

"Hey! I like his long hair."

"He does have beautiful hair," I agreed. "As for the car, I'll arrange a bank transfer for the full book value, no discount, plus I'll get you guys some souvenir T-shirts."

"Have fun driving around LA with Sir Drake Cheshire. Don't let him bite you on the neck. Or anywhere else."

We said goodbye, and I grabbed the comfy-looking jeans from the rolling rack.

I stared down at them in my hand.

What was that thing Adrian had yelled at the phone? *Not today, Satan!* Had he been referring to me, or to Nisha?

After careful consideration, I decided he had to have meant Nisha.

Chapter 6

The jeans were as comfortable as they looked.

I found Bernard in the kitchen and congratulated him for getting the right size.

"Where's the boss?" I asked.

"He's with trainer number two," Bernard said. "It's normal for him to do a workout first thing in the morning."

"This can't be normal," I said.

Bernard replied, "We all do what we must do to fulfil our roles in life. How would you like your coffee? A little birdie told me you enjoy dark mochas, so I took the liberty of picking up an assortment of chocolate mixers."

"You did? I owe you big time. Anything you want, just ask."

He smiled and prepared me a gorgeous mocha.

I thanked him and took the mug out to the back yard. I settled into a lounge chair next to the pool. A light breeze stirred up some fallen pink bougainvillea blossoms and blew them into the pool.

I had just taken two sips of my heavenly mocha when Dalton came out and found me.

He had apparently finished his morning workout, showered, and put on a casual outfit. His thick black hair was still wet. He wore a pair of jeans and a black T-shirt that hugged the muscles he'd just pumped. The guy was only halfway through his fast, but he looked camera-ready to my eyes.

"Let's hit the road," he said. "It's LA, so there's always traffic, but this time of day isn't so bad."

"But I've only had two sips of my mocha," I said.

He grabbed the mug from my hand and held it over a bougainvillea plant pot as he gave me a mischievous look.

"Don't you dare," I said. "Don't dump my mocha. I'll take it with me on the road."

"And spill it in my car? No way."

"I promise not to spill. I'll ask Bernard to throw it in a travel mug."

Dalton wrinkled his nose. "What's a travel mug?"

I got up, grabbed the mug, and gave him a dirty look. "Your father was a truck driver. You know darn well what a travel mug is."

He grinned.

I went to the kitchen and rummaged around until I found an entire cupboard of untouched travel mugs, all promotional items from movie screenings and other events.

We went to the garage, where Dalton told me to pick which car I wanted to use that day.

"I don't understand," I said. "Most of these are sports cars. Won't it be crowded with three of us in there?"

Confusion flickered across his face for a moment. "Ah. You think Bernard drives me everywhere."

"Doesn't he?"

"Only when I'm traveling, and it's just to give him something to do on the road, when he's away from the house and all the house duties."

I gave my head a shake. "Weird. My brain's recalculating now, like when you're driving and you take a wrong turn, and the navigation system has to figure out a new route." I gave my head a second shake. "Okay. Got it. Bernard is more of a butler when he's here, and a chauffeur when you're on the road. Is there anything else about his duties I should know about?"

Dalton smirked. "He doesn't bathe me, if that's what you're getting at."

I rolled my eyes.

"Though I could use some help scrubbing my back..."

I lifted my chin and looked over the cars. "That one looks fun," I said, pointing to a bright-yellow convertible.

"Good choice. My producer gave that to me for my birthday last year."

"Lucky you," I said. "My old boss at the bookstore sent me a fruit basket, except it wasn't even a real fruit basket. It was just pears in a crate. He thought he was so clever, too."

We walked toward the yellow coupe. "That's not very clever," Dalton said. "He should have sent peaches."

"They weren't in season, I guess."

Dalton licked his lips. "Pears are nice, too, but they're only ripe for about a day. They go from rock-hard to mush in no time."

"I know, right!" I grinned at Dalton. It was such a minor thing—agreeing about the downsides of a box of pears—but it still felt satisfying to connect with him on a low-stakes issue.

Adrian, by comparison, hadn't agreed with me about the pears. I'd had my twenty-third birthday in November, while we were dating, and he'd stubbornly eaten all the pears even after they'd passed their peak. With each mushy, mealy bite, he'd tell me how good the pear was, and that I was too fussy for my own good.

But that was Adrian. His contrary nature would be some other woman's problem now. I was with Dalton, who agreed with me about pears and probably about all sorts of things.

I settled into the passenger seat of the yellow car, looked around, and said, "Nope. I'm changing my choice. I don't see any cup holders for my travel mug."

Dalton waggled his eyebrows. "Or so it would seem," he said ominously. He reached in front of me, grazing my knee as he did, and pressed a hidden button, and a tray folded out in front of me, airline style.

"Wow," I said, as much about the folding tray as about the fireworks he'd set off in me simply by grazing my knee. "That's really... something."

"What can I say?" He rubbed his fingers together. "I've got the magic touch. All sorts of surprises happen when you grope around and find the right spot." He rested his palm on my knee.

I cleared my throat and gently removed his hand.

He chuckled and started the ignition. The car purred as we waited for the garage door to open.

I took two more sips of my mocha, and we were off.

As we rolled through his posh neighborhood, Dalton listed off the names of celebrities who were his neighbors.

He went quiet when we rolled past the treatment center he'd checked himself into the previous year for anxiety. A trio of horses ran alongside the car until they reached the end of their fenced pasture.

After a few minutes, I said, "This is nice."

He replied, "This is nice."

I took out my phone and snapped some pictures. "Don't worry," I said. "I'm not posting any of these online."

"I wouldn't mind if you did," he said.

"I'd rather not have the whole internet know I'm here with you. I like that it's our little secret."

"You know it won't stay secret for long." He snuck a glance over. "I've talked to my publicity people already and given them a heads-up."

"What did you say?"

"I told them that I would be spending some time with a certain curvy underwear model, and that I would try not to let her drag me into any compromising situations, such as running naked through the woods."

"That was all you," I said, faking indignation. "You're the trespasser. You!"

"Nobody would have paid for those security photos if it had been me on my own."

"You're so bad."

He chuckled. "That is my brand."

"So, what's the general plan for today?"

"Mostly sightseeing," he said. "I'll show you some of my favorite places, and, if we have time, I'd like to drive by some potential investments."

"Investments, as in real estate?"

"Yes," he said. "It's all quite boring, so I might do it another day and not drag you along. My financial advisor wants me to shift some assets into local properties."

"That doesn't sound boring at all. It's a good idea. My boss at the bookstore, Gordon Olivier, has made a fortune investing in Baker Street."

"Smart guy," he said. "Don't you mean your former boss?"

"Right. My *former* boss. I guess this whole unemployment thing will take some getting used to."

"Something tells me you'll do just fine. Peaches Monroe can handle anything life throws her way."

I smiled at him.

We drove on in a relaxed silence.

The drive along the coast was every bit as beautiful as I'd expected, based on having seen it in various movies.

We stopped in Santa Barbara for breakfast.

Well, I had breakfast, and Dalton smelled my croissant. (Not a euphemism.) He did order a black coffee, at least, which gave him something to do on his side of the table while I ate.

I'd worried about the situation feeling awkward—me eating while he was fasting—but it was fine. No, it was better than fine. Since I had my mouth full, he had to fill in the conversation. He opened up and started telling me stories about his dad—the one who'd raised him—and how Mr. Deangelo used to bring home unique souvenirs from his longer truck routes.

"Growing up, I assumed every kid had a drawer full of dirty calendars and shot glasses from every state," Dalton said. "My mother didn't think the gifts were appropriate, but it made my dad happy."

"He sounds like an interesting guy," I said. "I'm sorry I won't get to meet him."

Dalton looked away. "That's life."

"I guess I can't complain to you about my dad's irritating habits without sounding ungrateful. I know I'm lucky to still have him around."

"How is your dad, anyway? I should have made more of an effort to talk to him at the resort, but after he walked in on us in the hot tub, I couldn't look him in the eyes. Is he mad that you're here with me?"

"I don't know. I've only talked to my mom so far. If he is mad, he'll get over it." I added more butter to my croissant.

"Your dad sure is hairy," Dalton said.

I was so surprised by the frank assessment of my father's body hair, I spat croissant crumbs across the table.

Dalton grinned and dodged the spray. "And his chest and back hair is so *red*. He's like an orangutan."

"Stop it," I said, barely able to keep the half-chewed food in my mouth. "He's my *father*."

"Are you sure about that? Have you checked with the local zoo?"

I pleaded with him to stop before I choked, but he wouldn't.

"If Peter's looking for some acting work on the side, I could talk to some friends in casting," Dalton said, gravely serious. "Next month, they're shooting a Planet of the Apes spinoff."

I tried very hard to swallow my food without dying.

Dalton said, "With the money the costume department will save on red hair bodysuits, they can double the budget for spaceship CGI."

"Nooo," I cried, because I was literally crying from laughter by that point.

Dalton took out his phone and began filming me laugh-crying, which only made it worse.

The waitress came over and inquired if I was choking and required the Heimlich maneuver.

Dalton explained to the woman matter-of-factly, "She's just a little riled up because she got some upsetting news. Her father is an orangutan."

The waitress patted me on the shoulder. "It'll be alright, honey," she said sagely. "We've all got family secrets."

Chapter 7

After an entire vacation's worth of sightseeing in Los Angeles, we took the coastline drive back to Dalton's house in Malibu.

The sun was setting, and the ocean view was even more spectacular than it had been in the morning. We stopped at a lookout to take pictures of ourselves wearing the safari-themed hats we'd picked up earlier.

As we pulled up to Dalton's security gate, dark was settling around us. The landscape lights flicked on, giving the home a completely different night look. It looked even bigger and more elegant than it appeared in the day.

I complimented the house, and he shrugged it off.

"Your whole life is incredible," I said. "I get it now. I really do."

"You do?" He shot me a quizzical look.

"The house. The cars. Everything. Starting right now, I'm not going to say another word about your choices. No more questioning your fasting or your insane workout schedule. You have to take care of your investment in yourself, for your career. Looking around, it's abundantly clear that you are making all the right choices in your life."

"Thanks," he said hesitantly. "I'm not that materialistic, though. I don't think so. I truly do love my work. I love acting, and it just happens that all this stuff comes along with it."

"I love my work, too. Or at least I did. Working at the bookstore was amazing. But I'm twenty-three now, and all I have to show for myself is what you see in front of you."

The car was stopped for the gate, so he turned and looked me over. "Nothing wrong with that."

"True, but besides all of this, the only other thing I had was a job that was easily filled with a single phone call. I bet most of the customers won't even notice I've been replaced by Riley."

"Don't be so hard on yourself. Twenty-three is nothing. You're still young. And what about the modeling? I know you've only done one campaign so far, but I'm sure you could spin that into something bigger."

I looked around at the glowing house and perfect landscaping. "Why would I ever work hard at anything if I can just kick back and enjoy the fruits of *your* labor? Perhaps my true calling is being a lifestyle sponge."

Dalton nodded in agreement as he drove the car up the driveway and into the garage.

"That was a joke," I said. "I don't want to sponge off you."

"Why not? I've got more than enough for both of us. And Bernard gets bored just looking after me. He's delighted to have you here." Without taking his gaze off the garage parking spot, Dalton dropped one hand on my knee. "As am I," he said. "Delighted."

"I *am* rather delightful," I agreed.

"You're a better treatment for my anxiety than anything I've ever tried, by a factor of ten."

"I'm your therapy pet."

He turned off the ignition. "Are you?" He looked at me, his emerald-green eyes burning.

The heat of his gaze made my skin burn. I pretended not to have heard him. He had to be talking about whether or not I'd be sharing his bed with him later. I wanted to, but I couldn't. Not until I'd made things final back home with Adrian.

He leaned over, put his finger under my chin, and turned my face toward his. "Peaches, are you mine?"

"Not... tonight," I managed to say. "We're taking it slow, remember?"

"Remind me why we're taking things slow."

"Because it's what I want."

He raised an eyebrow. "Is it?"

I stared into his eyes. I could feel my resolve slipping away by the second.

And then someone's stomach growled. It wasn't mine.

Dalton winced. His stomach growled again.

He released my face and pulled back over to his side of the car. "Sorry about that," he said. "Whenever I'm fasting, the hunger flares up at mealtimes. When we pulled into the garage, my eyes told my stomach that we were home, and now my stomach thinks it's time to eat."

I reached over and poked him in the stomach. "Nice try," I said sternly. "No dinner for you. Not tonight." I shook my finger at Dalton's stomach. "Sorry, stomach. This is one of the many sacrifices you have to make so that I can live in the lap of luxury."

Dalton gave me an uncertain look. "It doesn't sound very fair when you put it like that."

"It's only temporary," I said, looking to his face instead of his stomach. "We can trade off. One day in the future when I'm making buttloads of money, it can be your turn to kick back and get comfortably plump. You can keep acting, but in roles where you don't have to be shirtless and emotional. That rules out most blockbusters, but I'm sure you'll think of something. Maybe you can write your own starring vehicle. Another independent flick, but better than the last one."

"Hmm." He frowned. "I wouldn't mind cutting back to just one personal trainer."

"Then it's a deal." I offered him my hand. "I'll take care of the bills, and you'll make the greatest indie flick ever."

He shook my hand warily.

Looking down at our hands, he said, "You know what? I've had a lot of fantasies about having you here in California with me, taking day-long dates, but none of those dates ended in a handshake."

"I'm full of surprises," I said, and I jumped out of the car before the handshake could lead to anything else.

Chapter 8

Tuesday, January 3rd

I woke up in my guest bedroom—alone again, unfortunately—and resolved that I would break up with Adrian Stromquist that day, no matter what.

I called every single person we had in common.

Nobody would help me ambush him.

A few people told me I was being mean to Adrian, and that I owed him an in-person breakup.

Adrian's mother made the most hurtful comment of all. "I'm not mad at you, dear," she said. "I'm just disappointed."

The closest I got to success was with Sunshine Banks. She said she'd be happy to sneak into my bedroom while Adrian was sleeping so she could photograph the two of them in a compromising pose, which I could use as emotional blackmail against him, except she'd recently started dating someone, so she couldn't.

I tossed my phone aside, defeated.

Then I grabbed it again and began calling lawyers.

Unfortunately for me, most lawyers have excellent call screeners. I couldn't get past their receptionists.

I was looking up phone numbers for escort services when there was a tap on my door.

"Don't come in," I yelled at the door. "I'm naked."

I wasn't naked. I was wearing silk pajamas. I was, however, surrounded by empty wrappers from the treats that had been in a welcome basket from the personal shopper. I hadn't noticed the stash the previous days, because it had been tucked in with the bath products. I'd made short work of the goodies.

From the other side of the door, a young man with a squeaky voice said, "I've seen you naked plenty of times! You don't scare me!" The door burst open, and in came my best—and only—friend in LA, Mitchell Dalhouse. His last name was pronounced *dollhouse* but spelled D-a-l-h-o-u-s-e.

He screamed in delight as he launched himself at me on the bed.

I'd been expecting Mitchell, but not for another half hour. We'd made plans to do a workout together in Dalton's home gym. Dalton had left before dawn to do a big hike for the final day of his cleansing fast. He wouldn't be home until late. He'd given me his blessing to invite friends over and enjoy the house. I only had one friend, so I'd invited him.

Mitchell and I hugged and rolled around on the bed, squealing like a couple of children. Bernard stood in the doorway, looking scandalized.

Eventually, we got ourselves calmed down. Bernard excused himself, and I took Mitchell on a tour of the house.

I'd met Mitchell the previous summer, during my first curvy underwear campaign. He was the brand manager for the clothing company. Brand manager was a job that I had believed was glamorous, until I learned he spent eighty percent of his days staring at spreadsheets. When he wasn't staring at spreadsheets, he was making pie charts about market share.

Mitchell Dalhouse was compact and slim, with straw-colored hair, big blue eyes, and a mischievous grin. He dressed, as he described it, "like a mid-Western accountant on vacation." He dressed for comfort, in sandals, cargo shorts, and a plaid, short-sleeved shirt. He claimed his job was to make the curvy women's underwear brand look good, so it didn't matter what he, a guy, wore. Besides escaping the office for the occasional outing to supervise photo shoots, he spent his days inside an air-conditioned office. His spreadsheets didn't care how he looked.

He made the requisite ooh and aah noises as I showed him around the place.

When we reached Dalton's workout room, Mitchell charged at the nearest piece of equipment and began tugging ineffectively at a pulldown bar.

"I think you're doing it wrong," I said. "For one thing, you're sitting side saddle. You need to straddle that bench."

"Straddle a bench? I'll do no such thing!" He released the bar and jumped away from the equipment as though stung by bees.

"Mitchell, you have to do it properly or your muscles won't get pumped. Or so I'm told."

"That sounds like a lot of work."

"But you came here for a workout," I said.

He wrinkled his nose. "I've got an idea for our workout. Let's *not*, and say we did."

His idea did have some merit. "I have zero problem with that. What are we going to do instead?"

He adjusted the collar of his lightweight plaid shirt. It was mostly blue, like his eyes. "Well, it's a weekday, which means I must be here on company time, doing official brand business, so we need to discuss the next campaign. Are you going to continue being our superstar model?"

"Yes."

"Are you going to rock the next campaign harder than ever?"

"You know I will."

"Good." He pretended to dust off his hands. "Business discussion accomplished. Let's take some post-business refreshments poolside. Does Jeeves know how to make pina coladas?"

"His name is Bernard, and he probably does. I haven't stumped him yet with a request."

Mitchell grabbed my arm and pulled me away from the gym equipment. "Then let's go. All this butch machinery is making me feel threatened."

I shook my arm free. "Your hands are awfully clammy."

"It happens when I'm around gym stuff. I can't hold onto anything heavier than a laptop. I'm hopeless. They're going to find out and kick me out of the Gay Gentlemen Club."

"I didn't know there was a Gay Gentleman Club."

"That's because the first rule is I'm not supposed to talk about Gay Gentleman Club."

"Is it fun?"

He stopped in his tracks and gave me a wide-eyed look. "Must I familiarize you with all of the completely accurate stereotypes about my people?"

"I'll take your word for it," I said, and we headed toward the pool.

* * *

Pool-side, we actually did talk about the brand.

Having been the highly visible spokesperson for the brand for several months, I had gotten plenty of feedback from female customers. Thanks to their suggestions, I had some ideas about cuts and colors.

It was too late to change the designs for the upcoming season, but my feedback did confirm some of Mitchell's theories about who was buying the clothes and why. The customers were women of every age, and they bought the underwear because it made them feel special.

"I'm almost jealous of the customers," Mitchell admitted. "I can't think of a single time I put on an item of clothing and felt transformed by it. Not since I took theater in high school, anyway. I liked wearing the nutcracker costume, with the tall furry hat."

"You would have been such a cute nutcracker!"

"I was." He sniffed. "I haven't felt that magic in years."

"That's because you dress like my dad, in your cargo shorts and plaid shirts," I said, sitting up straight on my poolside lounger. "I've got an idea. I can put you in touch with the personal shopper who picked out my look." I waved at my own ensemble. "Like this, but for a man." I'd changed out of the silk pajamas into a form-fitting jersey dress with a quirky animal-print belt.

"I'll think about it," he said noncommittally.

"You could always try tight jeans and a black T-shirt. It works for Dalton."

"Meow." Mitchell waggled his pale, straw-colored eyebrows. "I bet it does." He gave me a knowing look as he sipped his third pina colada.

"Don't be dirty," I said. "I told you on the phone. We're taking it slow, at least until I break up with Adrian."

"Ugh." Mitchell rolled his eyes. "Ugh," he said again, louder. He stood, handed me his pina colada glass, and dramatically fell backward into the pool, completely clothed.

He splashed me on the way in, then splashed me some more using his hands.

I squealed. "What's that all about?"

He put his hands around his mouth to form a megaphone and yelled, "You already broke up with Adrian!"

"I did not," I said.

He yelled back. "You did too!"

"Did not! At least not officially!"

He splashed me again. "You're just using Adrian as an excuse because you're scared of intimacy!" He was yelling quite loud.

I waved at him furiously. "Mitchell! Do you think you could scream about my fears of intimacy a little louder? There are people on the beach who didn't hear you."

He unbuttoned and peeled off his wet shirt as he treaded water. "I'm right, though," he said at a reasonable volume. He whipped his shirt through the air like a helicopter blade, then tossed it at me. His soggy shirt hit me in the face.

"You're going to pay for that," I said.

He grabbed a floating pool noodle and brandished at me. "Come here and fight me like a man."

"Don't think I won't." I unfastened my belt and pulled the dress off over my head. I was wearing matching underwear, which was basically as good as a bikini.

I grabbed another pool noodle and jumped into the water next to Mitchell. Fighting commenced.

We were mid-battle when Bernard ran out to see what the noise was about.

We paused, and the butler gave us a disapproving look. "I thought there might be coyotes attacking," he said. "You two nearly gave me a heart attack. You ought not scare me like that. I am over fifty, after all."

I opened my mouth to say something, but Mitchell whacked me on the back of the head with the pool noodle, and I had to pay him back by yanking off his cargo shorts and flinging them over the side of the hill.

Chapter 9

After my fun day with Mitchell, I relaxed in Dalton's home theater. I kicked back and enjoyed a personal screening of a new big-budget superhero movie. Then I enjoyed a nap in one of the luxurious recliners. It was dark in the home theatre.

I emerged from the home theater at nine o'clock, right when Dalton was getting home from his hike.

I ran to give him a hug in the entryway, but he begged me not to get too close. After a full day of hiking, he claimed he was filthy and stinky. He looked fine to me, but I held back at his request.

I stood off to the side while he groaned as he pried off one hiking boot and then the other. His hike must have been grueling.

He shot me a grimace and said, "Well? Did you have as much fun today as I did?"

"I don't have blood on my socks," I said.

"It's just foot blood," he said casually.

"That's not a thing," I said. "You're in need of medical attention."

"I'm fine." He reached out to steady himself with a railing and missed it completely. He was not fine.

"At least let me make you a sandwich," I said. "Bernard is off duty, but I've figured out where everything is."

"Don't," he barked. "I've got three hours left on my three-day fast."

"I know I said I wasn't going to question the sacrifices you make for your career, but come on. You look worse than my dad when he had to stay up two nights in a row because Elliot had croup."

"Three more hours," Dalton said, holding up four fingers instead of three.

"Fine. Three more hours. Sandwich at midnight."

He shook his head. "I'll be sleeping by then. But I promise to have breakfast with you in the morning. It will have to be a light meal, because my stomach will be sensitive, but I'll eat with you."

"Is it true that you might have a pants disaster after your first meal?" I looked away out of shame. "Mitchell told me some horror stories about the time he went to a yoga retreat. Has that ever happened to you after one of your fasts?"

Dalton didn't respond. The answer was all over his face. Yes, disaster-pants had happened. We would be staying close to the house the next day.

Dalton peeled off his bloody socks and said, "I'd better shower before I pass out. See you in the morning?"

"Not if I see you first." I pointed two finger guns at him and went *pow-pow*.

He gave me a weak smile. "I'm looking forward to it," he said with a raspy tone, then he turned and limped in the direction of his room.

I stood there a moment. My stomach growled.

The mere idea of him going to bed on an empty stomach after hiking all day made me so hungry that I immediately went to the kitchen and made myself a sandwich.

Then, since I wasn't in the mood for TV, I went to bed in my guest room.

When I hit the sheets, it was barely ten o'clock. That was early for me, plus I'd had a lengthy nap in the media room. I couldn't fall asleep.

As I lay there in the dark, I thought about what Mitchell had been yelling about in the pool.

Was Mitchell right? Was I using my lack of an official relationship termination with Adrian as an excuse to avoid intimacy with Dalton?

That couldn't possibly be true.

Why would a girl steal a car and drive all the way to California to be with a guy only to... not be with him?

And yet, there I was. Lying awake in a guest room, five doors away from Dalton's room.

By the time midnight rolled around, I'd been lying there thinking for a full two hours. I'd come up with a fantastic idea.

I got up, checked that I looked cute in my pajamas—of course I did—and tiptoed to the kitchen, where I made a second sandwich. I used lettuce instead of bread so that it would be low-carb, the way Dalton normally ate. It actually looked pretty good. I put the leafy "sandwich" on a tray along with some other snacks like soft cheeses and macadamia nuts. Then I tiptoed down the hallway to Dalton's bedroom.

I tapped on the door gently.

No response.

I opened the door and crept in.

Dalton was in bed, lying on his side, snoring softly.

I cleared my throat politely, the way Bernard did.

Still no response.

I set the tray on the bedside table and said softly, "I'll leave this here in case you wake up and feel hungry. It's just a little bit of food, so if you have a digestion apocalypse, it won't be a big one."

The room was dim, but I could have sworn he smiled.

He continued sleeping, snoring lightly.

"I have a confession to make," I said to the sleeping actor. "When I told you I wanted to take it slow, it was because I thought I had to based on a technicality. Remember Adrian? Of course you do. He's the guy whose name you pretend you can't remember."

Dalton didn't stir.

"The thing is, I didn't break up with him before I came down here. I know you were already split up with Harper, so you probably thought we were in the clear, but we weren't. Or at least I thought we weren't. But I was being delusional. I have broken up with Adrian, even if he says I haven't. Breaking up with someone isn't like getting married, where you both have to agree to it."

My mouth was dry. I took the cap off the mineral water I'd brought and took a sip before going on.

"I think what was going on is... maybe I was afraid of intimacy. Maybe, on some level, I was afraid of being with you. What if you're one of those guys who's all about the chase? What if, once you finally catch me, you don't want me anymore?" I held up one hand to stop him, even though he wasn't about to answer. "Don't say anything, because it doesn't matter. Our brains can't predict the future if they don't have enough information. How are we supposed to know how we're going to feel tomorrow or the next day until we actually get there?"

I finished talking and took a deep breath.

For the first time that evening, I was starting to feel tired. My eyelids were heavy. I had the overwhelming urge to be horizontal. Just for a minute, to rest my eyes.

There was plenty of room on the bed behind Dalton. I circled around and settled in next to him, above the covers.

The air conditioning came on and blew directly on me, making the back of my neck chilly. That wasn't comfortable.

I wriggled around, pulled up the covers, and settled in on my side. My knees were inches away from Dalton's legs.

A cozy feeling came over me. I wanted to touch him, to wake him up, but I also wanted to simply be there in the dark, enjoying the moment. If this wasn't an intimate moment, lying next to someone who was sleeping, I didn't know what was. And I wasn't scared at all. My heart was beating at a calm and steady pace.

Dalton took a breath and rolled over to face me.

His eyes opened.

I was so startled, I jerked my head back.

"Hello," he said.

I began to wriggle back. "Sorry I'm disturbing you. I'll go back to my room." My wriggling stopped. My body didn't want to go leave the warm bed, let alone go back to my room.

Dalton said, "There's something you should know about me."

"What's that?"

He wriggled closer to me and grinned, his teeth glinting in the dark. "I don't snore."

"Uh-oh," I said. "You were faking it? I should have known not to trust an actor. You heard my whole speech?"

"I think I was sleeping at the beginning, but I definitely heard the end of it. Why did you come in here?"

"I, uh, brought you a low-carb grass sandwich. I mean, a *lettuce* sandwich. I wanted to be sure you had something to nibble on."

He reached for me. "I could use something to nibble on."

I might have said something else, but he was kissing me, and my brain lost the ability to make words.

Chapter 10

I woke up in Dalton Deangelo's bed, alone.

I sat up and looked around. "Hello?"

He wasn't in the room.

I got up, found my pajamas, and pulled them on before going off in search of the handsome actor.

I found him in the hallway, pushing the rolling rack of my clothes toward me. I jumped out of the way just in time to avoid being trampled.

As he passed by, I held my hand to my chest. "Who needs coffee to start your adrenaline when you can get chased around by your own clothes?"

The handsome man with the tousled dark hair paused to give me a quick kiss then continued pushing the rack. "You're moving in with me," he called over his shoulder.

I followed him. "You don't want me and all my stuff in your nice bedroom. I'm not the most tidy person."

"I'll get used to it," he said.

"But I saw your walk-in closet. It's already crammed with all of your clothes. Hey, I have a question for you. If your TV show clothes are at the studio, and all you wear are black T-shirts, why do you have so many clothes, anyway?"

He didn't answer my question. He walked past his closet and opened a second set of doors on the other side of the room, revealing a second walk-in closet. That one was completely empty. He rolled my cart in and dusted off his hands.

"Ooh," I said. "It's like magic. Whatever you need, this house delivers."

"You'll have to work hard to fill yours up," he said. "That should keep you busy for a while."

He wasn't joking. The closet was large. The rolling rack looked tiny in the spacious room.

I said, "It's great that you have an extra closet for my junk, but you can't possibly want me and all my toiletries in your bathroom."

"I don't," he said, then he opened another door. Beyond it was another bathroom, a mirror of the one I'd already seen. "His and hers," he said. "As it should be."

"I should have known."

"It's better that you didn't." He walked up to me and kissed me on the forehead. "It's more fun for me to surprise you."

"You sure surprised me last night," I said.

He raised an eyebrow. "You mean when I pretended to be sleeping, but then I wasn't?"

"Among other things."

He blinked. "Speaking of which, I should eat something so I have the energy to surprise you again. Will you excuse me for a quick shower before breakfast? I could have sworn I showered last night, but something must have happened in my sleep to make me sweaty."

I smiled. "You might have had some strange dreams. Come to think of it, I did hear you making some funny noises."

He gazed into my eyes. "The funny noises were all you. Maybe breakfast should wait. I'd like to find out if I can recreate the specific circumstances that led to the other ones."

I took him by the shoulders, turned him around, and pushed him toward his bathroom. "Shower, then breakfast, then we'll discuss... specific circumstances."

Laughing, he walked away, pulling his boxer shorts down as he did to give me a cheeky view. He glanced back over his shoulder to see if I was looking. I whistled and pretended I hadn't been.

I planned to shower as well, but first I popped into my walk-in closet to hang up some of my clothes and start planning my outfit for the day.

There was a polite knock at the bedroom door. The butler. I called Bernard in and explained to him that Dalton was in the process of moving me in, which must have been obvious, but I felt the need to say it.

Bernard took a hanger from my hands and said, "Allow me, Ms. Monroe. This is my department."

I thanked him, and we took a minute to discuss how I'd like my closet to be organized. Well, he made suggestions, and I agreed.

I was about to hit the shower when Bernard said, "By the way, congratulations for finally breaking up with Mr. Stromquist."

"About that," I said, squirming on the spot. "I haven't actually spoken to him, but it's okay because I don't need to. Adrian's a big boy. He knows what's going on."

Bernard nodded curtly. "I understand. It's about what's best for you."

"Ouch," I said. "What's best for me? Way to make me feel like the most selfish person on the planet."

He gave me a blank look. "One person's selfishness is another person's boundaries. It's all a matter of perspective."

"Exactly," I said. "See? You get it. I'm drawing boundaries. Adrian doesn't have any say in what I do with my life. The idea that I had to get his permission to date someone else... it's preposterous. I'm nobody's property."

Bernard didn't say anything.

My own words rang in my head. *I'm nobody's property.*

It suddenly struck me that I was in Dalton's mansion, standing inside the room-sized closet he'd rolled my clothes into without asking, talking to his servant, and that I had zero plans for myself beyond a shower and breakfast. I was just the picture of independence, wasn't I?

I cleared my throat and looked away. "Well, I should be hitting the shower now. I wouldn't want Dalton to beat me to breakfast and eat all the food."

Bernard replied, "We have plenty of—"

I waved a hand. "It was just a joke," I said.

The butler visibly relaxed then gestured to the clothes. "I'll have this all taken care of right away. You'll have your privacy for getting dressed. Breakfast will be ready when you are."

I thanked him again and went into my bathroom—my gorgeous, spacious bathroom that was even more luxurious than the one in the guest room—and got in my shower.

I hadn't been under the water long when I was interrupted by Dalton coming into the bathroom.

"What's the matter?" I asked. "Did you run out of hot water on your side?"

He opened the glass door and stepped in with me.

"Yes. I did," he said. "Isn't that odd? You'd think a place like this would have more hot water."

"You'd think," I agreed.

"Hand me that spongy thing. I'll get the parts you can't reach."

"I can reach all of my parts just fine, thank you."

He held out his hand. I gave him the loofah.

As he rubbed my shoulders, he said, "You're going to love what I have planned for you today."

"Does it involve leaving the bedroom area?"

He laughed. "Surprisingly, yes. We're going horseback riding at a neighbor's place."

"We are?"

"It's all arranged," he said. "But we do have a few minutes to spare." He kissed my shoulder.

Chapter 11

Once I'd finished my shower, no thanks to the "help" from Dalton, we enjoyed a nice breakfast together, flirting with each other over scrambled eggs, smoked salmon, cream cheese, and a dozen other delicious things. None of the breakfast items were as delicious as him. The breakfast was pretty great, though. I'd worked up an appetite for some reason.

After breakfast, we got into one of Dalton's other cars—a low-key sedan—and drove in the opposite direction we'd gone the previous day.

Half an hour further up the coast, we reached the Lazy Boots Ranch.

The owners were John and Marie Zimmermann. They were older, sixty-something, with gray hair and tight, tanned faces.

The four of us stood in front of a sprawling rustic rancher and did introductions in the sunshine.

"Your name sounds so familiar," I said as I shook John Zimmermann's hand.

He laughed and told me that it should, since his name ran across the screen before every episode of *One Vamp to Love*. John was the producer of that show, as well as a dozen other hits. Those long-running TV series were what had paid for the Lazy Boots Ranch, among other things.

As I realized who he was, I felt myself blushing three shades of red. I made a mental note to pinch Dalton later for not giving me more warning.

John's wife sensed my embarrassment and pulled me aside.

"Boys will be boys," she said. "Dalton didn't warn you about who you were meeting today, did he?"

"He did not," I said. "I'm not exactly the world's best schmoozer at the best of times, but that was really bad. Your husband must think I'm a bobble-headed bimbo."

Mrs. Zimmermann laughed. "There's nothing this town loves more than a bobble-headed bimbo, so that wouldn't necessarily be a bad thing!"

"Uh, thanks?"

"You're a beautiful girl, Peaches." She looked me over. "With a face like that, and a body like that, you don't ever have to remember a single name to get to where you want to go. You could forget your own name!"

"That's sweet of you to say, Marie."

She squeezed my arm. "Call me Mitzy. Nobody calls me Marie." She rolled her eyes. "I don't know why John insists on introducing me that way. I've been married to the man for a million years. You'd think he would have figured out a few things by now."

I shrugged. "Boys will be boys," I said, repeating her phrase back to her.

Mitzy found this hilarious and roared with laughter.

John Zimmermann, the most prolific TV soap opera creator of all time, who'd been chatting with Dalton, demanded to know what all the fuss was about.

"Never you mind," Mitzy said back at him. "Peaches and I are having girl talk. It's nothing that concerns you. Now, where is Wayne with the horses?"

Right on cue, a group of horses came trotting out from behind the house. They came toward us.

Leading the pack was a cowboy-hat-wearing man on a black horse—Wayne, presumably. He led four other horses, all saddled up and ready to ride.

I raised my hand and called out, "Dibs on the sturdiest one for me!"

Mitzy roared with laughter again. "You are hilarious!"

"Seriously, I need a sturdy horse," I said to Mitzy. "I'm the kid who was too big for the birthday party pony. I know I'm a model and everything, but I am a plus-sized model."

Mitzy looked me over. "You *barely* qualify as a plus-size model. I don't want to hear another word about sturdy horses from you, Little Miss Barely Qualified. You'll ride my horse, Cindy." She waved for Wayne to bring over Cindy, a palomino with a broad white blaze down the front of her face. "Cindy will take good care of you. Introduce yourself."

"Hello," I said to the horse.

"Like this," Mitzy said. She forced one of her hands up my T-shirt sleeve, rubbed my armpit with her hand, then brought the hand to the horse's nostrils.

Cindy sniffed my armpit smell off Mitzy's hand. The horse made a pleasant huffing sound, flaring her nostrils, and nodded.

"She likes the smell of you," Mitzy said. "You'll be perfect together. Trust me. I used to be one of the town's top casting directors. I know all about chemistry. If there's one thing about chemistry, it's that you can't fake it."

I didn't say anything. I could take a lot of things in stride, but I was in shock from the unique experience of Mitzy rubbing my armpit.

Mitzy jumped on one of the other horses—a gray-maned white horse. She hopped on as easily as a regular person might throw their leg over a low stool. Then she gave me an expectant look.

I walked alongside Cindy, patting her reassuringly, then put my right foot in the stirrup.

"Wrong foot," Mitzy said. "Try the left, unless you want to ride backwards."

"I usually do ride backwards," I joked. "But it's been a while, so I'll try it the regular way today."

I put my left foot in the stirrup, grabbed the pommel, and flew up onto the horse the first try.

"Look at you," Mitzy said with a whistle. "You're a natural cowpoke!"

"Three cheers for muscle memory," I said. "I used to ride a bit when I was a teenager."

"Then you should have no problem keeping up," Mitzy said. "Let's go!"

Dalton, John, and Wayne were already leading the way on their horses.

Dalton shot a look back over his shoulder and gave me a thumbs-up. I might have flubbed the introduction with his boss, but I was making up for it with my impressive horse mastery.

* * *

Hours later, back at Dalton's house, I groaned as I lowered myself onto a chair in the dining room. I'd kept up with the others on our ride, and both John and Mitzy had loved me, but my body was now paying the price.

Bernard arrived with our salad starter then disappeared again without a word.

I reached for my fork and groaned again from the movement.

Dalton raised an eyebrow. "Too much horseback riding today?"

"Either that, or whatever that was in the shower this morning. Who can say? All I know is my thighs are very cross with me, plus whatever these muscles are on my sides. How are there muscles here? I thought these were ribs."

Dalton grinned. "You'll get used to your new lifestyle."

"If it doesn't kill me first."

His eyes twinkled.

We dug into our salads. I'd never been a fan of microgreens, but the dressing was very good.

"You and Mitzy were chatting up a storm on the ride," Dalton said.

"It was all her," I said. "I asked her about what she did, now that she's retired from being a casting director, and she told me. Oh, boy, did she tell me. You know about all her charities?"

"Ah, yes. Mitzy is involved in several charities. At least five, I believe. John's just glad she's too busy to pester him about retiring. I think that man will work until the day he dies. He can't stop. When you're on top like he is, nothing compares to the game."

I remembered the pinch I owed him. I didn't dare lean over and strain my rib muscles, so I gave him the verbal part only. "You could have told me I was meeting *the* John Zimmermann. I grew up watching his shows."

"You did fine. How's the wine?"

I took a sip of the wine Bernard had paired with the dinner.

"Tastes like berries," I said. "Which is exactly how I like my wine." I wrinkled my nose. "Do you think I could get an ice cube for it?"

Dalton laughed. He must have thought I was kidding. Even Bernard, who'd come to check on us, snickered and muttered, "An ice cube," under his breath before leaving.

Dalton asked, "What did you think of my friends?"

"They're a fun couple. Incredibly down to earth. I guess it's true what they say. Hollywood people are just like regular people, except better."

Dalton nearly choked on his wine. "Richer, maybe, but not better." He took another sip, watching me carefully over the glass. "So, which of Mitzy's charities did she sign you up for?"

"None of them. I told her I was interested, but that I'd have to wait and see what my schedule is like after I get a job."

Dalton laughed. "A job. That's funny."

I frowned at him. "Mitzy thought I was joking, too. Why is that? Why wouldn't I get a job?"

"Why would you?"

"It's what people do," I said. "I have a strong work ethic. All the Monroes do. Are you saying I couldn't get a job around here?"

"That's not what I'm saying at all." He looked down at his salad, which was rapidly disappearing. The man didn't eat carbohydrates, but he did eat a lot of other foods, and he ate it quickly. "I support the idea of you finding something to do on weekdays."

"Yes," I said, losing my patience. "People call that a *job*."

"Then we're in agreement," he said.

I narrowed my eyes at him. We were?

He went on, "You should look for something that keeps you busy during the same hours I'm on set."

"Which is weekdays and some evenings, right?"

"Yes, but I never know which days I'll have to stay late, so it would be better if you didn't work any evenings."

"Hmm." I chewed my salad.

Dalton said, "There's a very good reason the 'ladies who lunch' meet up with each other on weekday afternoons. It's so that they can be at their husbands' beck and call weekends and nights." He grinned. "Like good little wives."

I paused, mid-chew. "Like good little wives? You had better be joking."

He blinked, pretending to be dead serious. "You should hang out with Mitzy some more. She'd be a positive influence. She'd get you trained right up. I hear from John that she's a very good little wife. More obedient than most."

"Now you've done it," I said, dropping my fork and pushing up imaginary sleeves. "Someone's going to get a double punch in the butt."

"I'd like to see you do that."

"You'll never see it, because the attack comes from behind."

He batted his dark eyelashes at me. "Sure, but you'll have to catch me first."

In a flash, he was up from the dining room table and running from the room.

I kicked off my sandals—I'd have better grip in my bare feet—and ran after him.

I chased him through the house.

By the time I caught him, I'd forgotten what I'd been worked up about, but I did deliver a couple of playful punches to his perfectly chiseled bottom.

He turned me over his knee and threatened to repay the abuse with a spanking.

One thing led to another, and Bernard had to reheat our dinner when we finally returned to the dining room.

Chapter 12

Wednesday, February 1st

One Month after my Dramatic Arrival in California

I hadn't made much progress on the job search—mainly due to not having sent out a single resume.

For the past three and a half weeks, I'd been busy setting up my full wardrobe, and, well, that was about it.

Yes, it's true. I spent three and a half weeks shopping for shoes, handbags, and clothing for all occasions. All on Dalton's credit card.

I did take a few breaks to hang out with my only friends in the state, who now included not just Mitchell, the brand manager, but Mitzy, who'd all but adopted me.

That Wednesday afternoon, I was wearing one of my new suits that I'd bought specifically for wearing to one of her charitable luncheons.

I walked into the restaurant where the lunch was taking place and scanned the room for my friend.

She spotted me first and rushed over.

Mitzy looked my chic new suit over and said, "Love the outfit, darling. All you need to finish the look is a string of pearls." She removed the pearl necklace from her own neck and fastened it around mine before I could say another word.

Then she grabbed me by the hand, hauled me over to some other women who could have been her clones, and introduced me. The last woman whose hand I shook was described as yet another of her "dear friends." Mitzy had a lot of dear friends.

When we got a moment alone again, I said to Mitzy, "I do enjoy our luncheons, but next time, can we meet up at your place and ride horses on the beach again?"

She roared with laughter. "You are too funny." She leaned in and sniffed my neck. "What is that scent?"

"It's my skin," I said. "That's just what I smell like. Please tell me you're not going to rub your hands in my armpit again."

She laughed lightly and grabbed a bottle of perfume from her purse. She blasted me on the neck then smelled me again.

"Just as I suspected," she said.

"Is that all I am to you, Mitzy? A perfume sampler?"

"It's your pheromones I was smelling," she said. "You're in love." She held up the tiny spray bottle. "I had to cover up the scent before the other women smelled it on you and attacked. They're like a pack of hyenas."

"Your *dear friends* attack women for being in love?"

She raised her eyebrows. "They do, and not from the front," she said. "Trust me. You must always wear perfume when you're meeting women like these in a group like this. As self-protection."

"Good to know," I said. "Good to know."

* * *

Two hours later, I was driving myself back to Malibu in the car I'd bought from Noah.

I called Mitchell Dalhouse on speakerphone.

He answered in a fake deep voice, "Bob's Lumber. We've got wood." It was how he answered the phone when he saw that it was me.

"You won't believe what happened today with Mitzy's dear friends who lunch," I said breathlessly.

"Did she smell your armpits again?" Mitchell was back to his adorable squeaky voice.

"Not exactly. She sniffed my neck, then she doused me in perfume so that the other hyenas didn't get jealous of my, um, youthfulness." I didn't want to admit the being-in-love thing just yet.

"Interesting," Mitchell replied. "You know what? That actually explains a lot about those women. How was the lunch? Don't tell me it was one of those events where they only serve finger foods. We hate that."

"We do hate that," I agreed. "But there was food at this one, and it wasn't bad."

"Quiche?"

"Oh, Mitchell. It's always quiche. You know that. Gluten-free quiche."

"I'd kill for some quiche right now."

"What are you doing? How's work?"

"It's the most fun ever," Mitchell said flatly. "I had to put in eyedrops an hour ago, Peaches. When I close my eyes, I still see spreadsheets. I think they're burning into my retinas permanently."

"Yikes," I said. "That doesn't sound healthy."

"I don't mind so much. Sometimes I get down on Wednesdays because the weekend's so far away."

I made a noise to indicate that I totally understood, even though I hadn't realized it was Wednesday until he'd mentioned it.

"I know," he said brightly. "Why don't you come over again for dinner? Byron is making ragu." Byron was Mitchell's husband. The two had been married for a year and were in the process of adopting a dog. They were still early in the process. As in still at the point where they would just randomly mention to each other how nice it might be to have a dog.

Did I want a weeknight dinner with Mitchell and Byron? I shoulder-checked and changed lanes while I was thinking about Mitchell's offer. I didn't want to turn around and head back into traffic again, as good as Byron's cooking was. I was quickly learning that, thanks to heavy Los Angeles traffic, a person's zip code really did affect their desirability as a casual hangout.

I answered, "Thanks for the offer, but I've already been at your house for dinner five times in the last three weeks, which is way too often for a third wheel."

"You're not a third wheel."

"I know, but you guys are newlyweds. You need your space. Plus I think Byron's jealous of our relationship."

Mitchell sighed. "You are... not wrong. My Byron is a big, jealous beast. I love him so much, though."

"You know who else was jealous? Adrian."

"Ugh. I am not in the mood to hear about Adrian. You need to let it go."

I should have let it go, but I couldn't. "He still won't talk to me," I complained. "I got his new phone number, and he immediately blocked me."

"So? What do you want from the guy? It's very clear to anyone with eyes that you've moved on. What more do you need?"

"I'd like a little something called *closure*. Just because I'm down here—"

I was cut off by Mitchell saying, "Nope, nope, nope. Just hearing his name brings up stomach bile. I can't do it today. I'd rather conduct an audit on last month's cash flow. If you knew how tedious that was, you'd understand the depth of my aversion to discussing the whole Adrian situation."

"Sorry," I said. "I guess it is old business."

A minute passed.

"Don't pout," Mitchell said. "I can hear you pouting. Don't give yourself pout wrinkles. We can't have you looking sad in the next campaign. Put a smile on your face and cheer up. The sun will come out tomorrow, because the sun always comes out in California."

"That's not true. There was that rain shower yesterday."

"But did it rain *all* day?"

"No."

"Exactly." There was static on his end of the call. I heard someone come by his desk and ask a question. After Mitchell answered, he came back on the line and said, "I should get back to work. Thanks for calling. Talk again soon. Love ya."

"Love ya right back," I said.

* * *

When I got back to the house, Dalton wasn't home yet.

I checked my phone.

There was a message from his on-set assistant, advising me that "DD"—her nickname for him—would be working late.

I went to the kitchen to see if I could help Bernard with dinner. Well, I offered to help, but I knew he wouldn't let me, so really I was just there to find out what we were having.

The butler said, "Since Mr. Deangelo will be working late and eating on set, I thought I'd make pasta."

"Real pasta made from wheat flour, or that pretend stuff you make out of vegetables?"

"Real organic pasta, imported from Italy."

"Score," I said. "That sounds so good, in fact, I won't even ruin my appetite with these vegan granola bars I got in my gift bag today." As evidence, I turned the granola bars over to Bernard to add to our snack cupboard.

* * *

Since I would be eating dinner alone—Bernard didn't eat with his employers, except on rare special occasions such as New Year's Day—I called Nisha.

I used a tablet to put her on video call, setting her up in the spot across the table from me, where she'd have a view of yours truly as well as the ocean behind me.

A pretty young woman with dangling silver earrings and short black hair appeared on the screen.

"Your hair," I said, surprised by the sight of my best friend on the screen. Nisha had progressively been cutting her hair shorter and shorter over the past few months. It had gotten shorter still—a pixie cut.

"It's so different, right?" She rubbed her hand over what was barely more than stubble. "I just love the feel of it," she said breathily.

"That's odd. Noah's man-bun gets longer every day, and your hair gets shorter. Is that a cosmic balancing thing?"

She replied, "It's all part of my plan to have my hair be as low maintenance as possible."

"But why?"

"A few reasons," she said, making a coy expression.

I lifted a forkful of pasta to my mouth. "I'll be eating, and you'll be talking now. Go."

She took a big, excited breath. "First of all, Noah took the car sale money you sent him, and he bought a Volkswagen camper van. Instead of doing a regular wedding, we decided to get married at City Hall and take six months off work to go on a road trip around the country."

I swallowed my pasta and waved my fork at the screen. "You can't do that. What about releasing the doves? The photo booth with the alpaca? The Peruvian food that all your aunties will complain about?"

"Too late," she said, wrinkling her nose. "We actually already did it on Monday. I'm married!"

I was stunned. It was a good thing I was sitting down, or I might have fallen over. "You got married without me? Alone?"

"Adrian was there. Plus we only needed one witness."

"How dare he!" I felt my pulse rushing in my ears as my blood pressure increased. "Adrian can't be your witness! You're *my* best friend!"

"But you weren't here, and he was," she said.

"It isn't right," I said.

There was a blur behind her. Someone had walked by quickly.

I grabbed the tablet screen with both hands. "Who was that walking behind you? Is Adrian there? Point the camera at him right now!"

The smile fell off Nisha's face. "Relax, psycho. It was just Noah."

Noah's head popped in beside Nisha's. "Hi, Peaches. Is that a tan? Wow. It must feel so good to have a tan in February."

"It's okay," I said without enthusiasm. "Congratulations on getting married without me there."

Noah's head bobbed. "Thanks, dude." He murmured something in Nisha's ear.

She squirmed. "Not yet," she said to him.

"What's going on?" I demanded.

The sharpness of my tone caused her head to snap. She stared at me with wide eyes.

I asked again, "What's going on there?"

She leaned in, filling the screen with the top of her face, and said, "Listen, it sounds like we've both had a long day today. It's not really a good time for me to chat. I don't have a butler to serve me dinner. I still have to make something to eat. How about we talk again soon?"

"Sure," I said, feeling bad about my behavior, but not bad enough to actually apologize.

We ended the call and I ate my pasta alone. Truly alone.

* * *

When Dalton finally got home at nine o'clock, I blubbered to him about how Nisha was moving on with her life and I wasn't a part of things anymore.

We were in the room where Dalton liked to relax after a long day. The room had no television, just speakers for music. There was a long sectional sofa as well as several mats for stretching out on the floor. Dalton was reclining on a mat, stretching his legs.

"It's not fair," I said, on the verge of a full-blown tantrum. "I've only been gone a month, and she went and got engaged and *then* married. Without me!"

"That was fast."

"I know, right?" I stretched out on another mat next to him and let out a long sigh. "It's not fair."

"You feel left out," he said sympathetically.

"I do feel left out," I said. A minute passed, and I added, "But I suppose I was the one who left."

Dalton didn't say anything.

After another minute, I'd cooled down completely.

I said, "But enough of my complaints. I'm done with my day, unless you want to hear about Mitzy comparing the ladies who lunch to hyenas."

"Hyenas," he mused. "Have you ever seen a hyena give birth? It's quite violent."

I snorted. "Childbirth is pretty violent."

"With hyenas, it's a touch more dramatic. You see, the females—" He stopped himself. "Never mind. I don't mean to change the subject away from your day. I hear what you're saying about your friend Nisha, and I want you to know I completely understand."

I propped myself up on my side and stared into his eyes. "You do?"

"This exact same thing happened to me when I got the job playing Drake Cheshire."

"You lost your best friend?"

"No." He gazed over my shoulder at nothing. "I lost a whole group of friends. All of the actor buddies I'd come up with, they turned on me. Once upon a time, we had been a tight-knit group." He chuckled. "We used to give each other such a hard time. We were brutal with our notes." He rubbed his chin. "Then, when I started working on a successful show, everything changed. You'd think they would have been *more* appreciative of my notes, since I actually knew what I was talking about. But they took everything the worst possible way. Then, when I stopped giving feedback, they'd accuse me of thinking I was too good for them."

"That's awful," I said. "You couldn't win, could you?"

"For a few years, I stubbornly kept hanging out with a few of the guys. Eventually, I realized it was always me calling them, and never the other way around." His face contorted into bitterness. "And they'd only go out for drinks or dinner if I promised ahead of time to pick up the tab."

I put my hand on his arm. "I'm so sorry to hear that. But don't feel bad about losing those jerks. It just goes to show you they weren't your friends in the first place."

Dalton shook his head and rolled onto his back, avoiding eye contact. "People always say that, but it's not true. I'm not delusional. I know what a friend is. They *were* my friends, and then they weren't."

I didn't say anything.

He went on. "It's like when one person in the group gets into a self-destructive lifestyle, with drugs or gambling, and the others gradually push that person out because even though they love the person, they can't abide the addiction. It was the same thing with me, except it was my success they couldn't live with."

"Huh," I said. I could understand how success could drive people apart in a way that even failure couldn't.

We were both on our backs, staring up at the ceiling. The chill-out room really was good for chilling out.

After a few minutes, I said, "Life isn't easy. It's almost like everything good comes with an equal cost."

He reached over blindly and caught my hand in his. "Sometimes it feels that way." He squeezed my hand. "But not all the time. For example, I've got you, and there's nothing bad about that."

Without hesitation, I said grimly, "Give it time."

He squeezed my hand. "You're only saying that because you had a long day, and you missed me."

"I did miss you."

After a moment, he said, "We should send Nisha and Noah a wedding gift."

I snorted. "But they didn't even invite us to their dumb City Hall wedding."

"Exactly," he said. "If we send them a really lavish gift, then they'll feel bad. The bigger the gift, the worse they'll feel."

"You... are... diabolical."

"What can I say? Being diabolical comes naturally to me after all these years playing a vampire on TV."

I turned to face him and was struck by a thought.

I love him.

It wasn't just his beautiful face, or how much he cared about my feelings. It was everything. I loved that diabolical man.

The next day, we sent Nisha and Noah a wedding gift. It was a small camping and storage trailer they could tow behind their Volkswagen van. It was brand new and cost more than ten old vans.

Chapter 13

Dalton was at work, as usual. The studio had been in full production mode since the second week of January.

I had nothing to do.

Rather than sitting around waiting for his assistant to text me with the news that DD would be working late again, I decided to find something productive to do.

For an hour, I followed Bernard around the yard, trying to badger him into telling me embarrassing stories about his boss. He refused to divulge any information, as usual.

I went back inside and consulted my phone.

Mitzy Zimmermann had invited me to one of her luncheons with the hyena ladies who wore animal print dresses.

I texted her back to politely decline, promising to make it to the next one instead.

If only I had plans with another person my age.

The closest person was Mitchell, but he couldn't play hooky from work on another weekday.

I scrolled through my contact list.

I did know one other person in their twenties in Los Angeles.

Josie Ranger. Dalton's half-sister.

I sent her a message asking if she was up to anything special that day, and if she was even in town.

She responded back immediately.

After a flurry of messages, we had a date set up for that day.

I freshened up my makeup, brushed my hair, and set out to meet her.

* * *

That Friday was sunny, as usual.

Josie Ranger and I walked down a street in West Hollywood. That was where Josie lived, in one of her father's spare apartments. I hadn't seen the interior yet because she'd met me in the lobby. I took that to mean I was still on probation for a full-time friendship position. Honestly, I didn't care. I was just happy to have something to do besides rack up Dalton's credit card.

Josie was looking chic in an oversized pair of sunglasses. Her pixie-cut hair had been trimmed and was nearly as short as my friend Nisha's new look. Josie wore a pair of worn-out denim overall shorts over a crop-top shirt emblazoned with the word *Hollywood*. I found it odd that someone who lived there would wear a T-shirt meant for tourists, but she explained to me that a great way to fly under the radar was to look like a tourist.

As we walked along the sunny sidewalk, window shopping, Josie said, "I'm so glad you got in touch today. I can't believe you've been living here for a month and we haven't hung out together until now."

"It was Dalton's idea," I admitted. "I kept complaining to him about Mitzy and the ladies who lunch, and he suggested I might enjoy spending time with someone my own age. He's the one who programmed your number into my phone."

"Thanks a lot," she said with a snort. "Way to make a girl feel wanted. It's nice to know you only called me because I fit your demographic."

I felt a lump rise in my throat. We'd been hanging out for all of ten minutes, each of them pleasant enough, but I'd said the wrong thing. Josie had thin skin, and things had taken a hairpin turn.

I quickly defended myself, saying, "Let's be honest, Josie. You can't blame me for not relishing the idea of hanging out with you, considering how we met."

She slid her sunglasses down her nose and gave me a withering look. "How am I the bad one here?"

"Come on," I said. "You know what I'm talking about."

She pushed her sunglasses up and stuck her nose in the air. "I've always been nothing but respectful toward you."

"Hah!"

We were passing by a flower shop with an outdoor display of bouquets and plants. It was quaint, like Gardenia Flowers back home on Baker Street. There was a green water hose snaking across the sidewalk, the spray nozzle dripping water on the pavement.

The hose gave me an idea.

Josie wasn't listening to what I was saying, but there was another way to get through to her. They say actions speak louder than words for a reason!

I stopped, picked up the hose and pointed it at Josie.

She froze on the spot and put both hands up. "Wha-what's going on?"

"What does it look like? I'm pointing a hose at you. What's your problem? I'm being *nothing but respectful* toward you. This is just the way people greet each other where I'm from."

She backed away slowly. "Oh," she said. "I remember now. Didn't we have some sort of joke thing with a hose when we met? Maybe it wasn't respectful, but it was pretty funny."

"I don't recall laughing."

She whipped off her sunglasses and glared at me. "Is that why you wanted to hang out with me today? For revenge? Over something that happened a whole year ago?"

I did the math in my head. "It was nine months ago."

"So? Who holds a grudge for nine months? You're crazy."

I shot off a short blast at her feet. "Maybe I am crazy," I said, bobbing my head from side to side. "There's no telling what I might do next."

She gaped at her wet sandals then gave me a horrified look. "I'll tell Dalton!"

"Relax," I said. "I'm not really going to soak you. Probably."

She frowned at me. "What do you want?"

"I'm just trying to make a point that I'm not the bad one. You're the bad one."

"I am *not* the bad one. You're the bad one."

I gripped the nozzle tighter. "The first time we met, Josie Ranger, you were skulking around, trying to take sneaky photos that you could sell for big bucks. That's not something good people do. When Dalton sprayed you with the garden hose on my front lawn, you were getting what you deserved. But when you sprayed *me*, that wasn't fair. I was an innocent bystander. Me, good. You, bad."

She took another cautious step back. "Maybe I have some regrets about that. But it's in the past. I've made amends. How many times do I have to tell you I'm sorry?"

I laughed hollowly. "How many times? Josie, I think if you'd said you were sorry to me, oh, *one single time*, I might have forgiven you." I switched the hose nozzle to my other hand and scratched my temple theatrically. "But I don't seem to recall those words coming out of your mouth."

"But I am sorry," she said.

"For what?" I channeled my father and said, "Are you only sorry you got caught?"

She shook her head. "I am... sorry I sprayed you with the hose."

"How about that other thing you did? When you sold off the photos of me running through the woods half naked?"

"I'm sorry about that, too," she said. "But you have to admit, that exposure was good publicity. If anything, you should be thanking me. It was because of those photos that you got the modeling—"

I blasted her in the midsection with the hose water.

She shrieked, looked around, and grabbed a nearby bucket of water that had been set out for dogs.

For a petite girl, Josie had a decent water-throwing arm. She blasted me with the dog-bucket water and followed up by pelting me with the bucket itself.

I, however, still had the hose. I let loose.

She sputtered under the spray and began yanking flowers from more buckets and throwing them at me.

Five minutes later, when the owner of the flower shop came out to see what the fuss was about, we were both drenched, covered in petals, and still flailing away.

The man yelled, "Arrêté!"

Josie and I froze and stared at each other.

The corner of Josie's mouth curled up. She looked me in the eyes and asked, "Is that man speaking French, or is my brain soaked with hose water?"

The man let out a burst of French. I was not fluent in the language, but it was very clear to me we were being sworn at.

Josie started to giggle, and then I did, too.

Together, we calmed down the French florist. He forgave us when Josie handed over her credit card and bought the entire display. She instructed the man to deliver the non-destroyed flowers to Dalton's house.

We walked away with our elbows linked so we could keep each other from falling down laughing.

The rest of the day went remarkably well.

We stopped by Josie's apartment to get dried off, then we spent the afternoon looking at her old photos and memorabilia from growing up as the daughter of Jocko Ranger, everyone's mom's favorite action hero.

A few hours in, Josie showed me her sobriety pin that commemorated how long she'd been clean of drugs and alcohol.

"A full year," I said. "That must be quite an achievement."

She swished her lips from side to side bashfully.

I put my arm around her. "I'm proud of you," I said.

It seemed like a weird thing for me to say, yet also appropriate. She was Dalton's half-sister, plus she was also a half-sibling to Garnet, a kid I'd worked with at the bookstore for ages. If Josie wasn't basically family, then who was?

Her eyes glistened, and she pulled away from me, clearing her throat and blinking away the emotion quickly.

"Yeah, well, I've had the one-year pin before and lost it," she said. "Don't make any bets on my continued sobriety."

She started putting away all the shoeboxes of mementos.

I sensed that our time together had reached its emotional peak. I didn't want to stick around for the inevitable point where we would get on each other's nerves again, so I thanked her for the fun day, left, and headed back up the coast.

I hit bad traffic, and the drive took two hours longer than expected.

On the plus side, I caught up on a couple podcasts. On the negative side, I finally fully understood the locals' complaints about the traffic. I missed Baker Street and being walking distance from everything I needed.

When I got to the house, I found that the flower delivery had beat me home. Every surface of the home was covered in bouquets and houseplants.

It was the perfect end to a great day.

The rest of February was similarly good.

It wasn't until March that the next big shakeup happened.

Chapter 14

Saturday, March 4th

(A Month Later)

Dalton's red-haired personal trainer was named Tyler. In addition to being a highly sought-after personal trainer to the stars, Tyler was also a smooth salesman. He'd managed to talk me into working out. For real.

"You'll love lifting weights," he'd said with confidence.

"I hate the gym," I'd said.

"Have you ever lifted weights?"

"No," I admitted.

"That's why you hate the gym. Most people treat going to the gym as punishment. They slack off all week, then do their weekend penance on the cardio machines. It's a waste of a good gym to not enjoy your time there. It's like going to church just for confession and not getting your spirit lifted while you're there." Tyler was an avid church-goer.

"I like having my spirit lifted," I'd said.

He'd intrigued me enough that I'd agreed to a sample workout back in early February. Since then, I'd had a weightlifting workout one day out of every week, which was a routine I could keep up with.

Tyler kept our sessions short and fun. I wouldn't say I loved it, but I didn't hate it.

That Saturday in March, on my fourth ever weightlifting workout, Tyler congratulated me on my work ethic as I struggled to do one more pulldown.

"Hah," I said. "I don't have a job, so I have to put my efforts into something."

"You're investing in yourself," he said. "One more."

"I don't have it in me."

"You wouldn't be sassing me off if you didn't have a little more fuel in the tank."

"I hate you," I said.

"Hate all you want. I get that a lot, and it bounces right off me."

I kept pulling. I did have one more rep in me, as it turned out. The pulldown bar was moving at a glacial pace, but it kept moving.

"There you go." He helped me with the final bit, using only his pinkie so I knew I was doing most of the work myself.

When the workout was finished, I said, "It's been almost a month now, and you haven't said anything about my weight."

"Why would I?" The red-haired man with the colorful tattoos all over his athletic arms looked genuinely confused.

"You're a personal trainer," I said. "When you look at someone like me, you must be imagining how much better I'd look if I lost some of this." I gave my hip a playful slap.

"Well, since you brought it up, there's nothing wrong with that," he said, pointing at my hip. "It's subcutaneous fat. Some people have more than others, but there's nothing wrong with it. I only talk about fat loss with my clients who have it here." He grabbed his own stomach through his shirt—not that he had anything to grab. "The dangerous fat is the kind that gets in around the organs," he explained, then he got out his phone to show me something.

For the next fifteen minutes, I got an unwanted talk about visceral fat and full-body scan imaging. He showed me Dalton's scan from a couple years back, then compared to now. I had never wanted to see my boyfriend's organs in that level of detail, but now that I'd seen his insides, I only loved him more.

I thanked Tyler for the workout and biology lesson, then I hit the shower.

After I'd finished showering, I got changed for my night out. Dalton and I were going to a comedy club with Mitchell and Byron.

I went off in search of Dalton. The man could be ready for public appearances in two minutes flat, but we did have to get going.

After searching half the house, I finally found Dalton in the chill-out room with Tyler. I thought he'd left after our session, but apparently he hadn't.

The red-haired trainer was sitting cross-legged on one of the mats, typing away on a laptop. There were sheets of computer printouts all around. At a glance, I knew the pages were from a script.

Neither of the guys looked up when I entered the room.

"What's going on here?" I asked. "Are you guys... running lines?"

Tyler quickly closed the laptop and gave me an embarrassed look. "Sorry," he said.

Dalton patted Tyler on the shoulder. "Don't be sorry, man." Dalton looked up at me and said, "Tyler's not just the best trainer around. He's also a talented screenwriter."

Tyler looked even more uncomfortable. He muttered something I didn't catch.

"He's really got something," Dalton said. "I've been giving him some notes on his project, and it's really coming together. This could be The One."

"The One," I repeated back. Like many TV actors, Dalton was always on the lookout for The One. That was the movie project that could elevate him from

TV star to movie star. All TV actors pretended they didn't care about the big screen, but each and every one of them was always secretly searching for The One.

Dalton picked up some nearby pages and said to Tyler, "We need a better name for the hero. Something that tells us more about him."

Tyler asked, "You don't like Jack?"

Dalton wrinkled his nose. "It sounds too much like Jocko. A certain Mr. Jocko Ranger would like it, but he's not getting anywhere near this."

"Oh, right." Tyler smacked his forehead and opened the laptop. He began typing furiously.

I checked the time. "Hey, maybe you can tell me more about this movie project on the drive."

Dalton gave me a blank look. "What drive?"

"We're going into the city to meet Mitchell and Byron at that comedy club. We're on the guest list. Why are you giving me that blank stare? It's been on your schedule for weeks, DD." Whenever I teased him about his busy schedule, I called him DD, channeling his on-set assistant.

"Oops." Dalton winced. "Would you hate me if I stayed here and you went without me?"

"I could never hate you," I said.

Dalton watched over Tyler's shoulder as he typed.

I stayed in the doorway another minute then asked, "Who's going to drive me home tonight if I've had a few drinks?"

"Call the car service," Dalton said. "Or stay over with Mitchell and come back in the morning."

I looked at Tyler, who gave me a guilty look.

I didn't move from the doorway. I'd really been looking forward to the night out with the four of us. Dalton and I had never done a couples' hangout with the boys.

I felt a pout coming on, but I managed to stop it.

After a moment, I was able to say, without sarcasm, "Good idea, babe. I don't need you to drive me. I'll just stick to sugary soft drinks."

I saw a disapproving look go across Tyler's face at the mention of soft drinks. He'd told me that sugary beverages were the leading cause of the wrong kind of body fat. It bothered him that I would drink them so quickly after his lecture. He wisely didn't say anything.

"Have fun with your writing," I said with sincerity, and left them to it.

I was proud of myself that I'd been able to put Dalton's needs ahead of my own. Who was afraid of intimacy? Not me.

Over the past two months that I'd been living with the man, I'd learned that he didn't have a lot of friends. It was no wonder he was still bitter about the acting friends who'd ditched him for being successful.

He had thrown a party at the house the previous weekend, but all the guests had been people from his TV show. Dalton was friendly with several of them —all actors and crew who had nothing but glowing things to say about the man—but as friendly as they were on set or at parties, they never called him on their days off.

This new development with Tyler, the personal-trainer/screenwriter, made me happy for Dalton. He was such an amazing guy, and he deserved more friends. Whether their screenplay worked out or not, it was good that they had a project.

I let myself into the garage, glanced over all the vehicles, then grabbed the keys for the old Mercedes that I still thought of as Noah's car.

On the drive toward the city, I listened to a self-improvement audiobook Josie had recommended. It was about sobriety and finding a higher spiritual calling, and also about breathing.

By the time I got downtown, I'd given up on the title and switched to a science fiction story about aliens invading the planet. The aliens were just looking for love! I hoped the screenplay Tyler and Dalton were working on was half as good, because it was a gripper!

I arrived at my destination right on time.

Much to my relief, the comedy club had valet parking, which meant I didn't have to hunt around for a spot. If I'd found one on my own, the Mercedes would be at risk for getting towed or run over by a street sweeper because I would have inevitably failed to decipher the hieroglyphics on the parking signs. Locals complained about LA parking and always getting towed for a reason.

The comedy club itself wasn't the famous one on Sunset Boulevard where every comedian who'd made it big in the last thirty years had gotten their start, their downfall, and their eventual comeback. Nor was it part of a corporate chain. It was, however, close to where Mitchell lived, and he had several friends who performed there regularly. Mitchell's husband, Byron, knew the owner from way back.

There was already a lineup behind the velvet rope.

I strode up to the doorman and gave him my name. I didn't get into the whole story about who knew whom.

"Peaches Monroe," the doorman said. He had a deep voice, an imposing build and a shaved head, but a friendly face. "I thought someone wrote that on the guest list as a joke, but you are..." He looked me up and down appreciatively. "No joke." Then he grinned, revealing gleaming teeth and the cutest dimples, which made his comment seem charming rather than lecherous. "With a name like that, you must have quite the act to go with it. I can't wait to hear your set."

"Oh, I'm not a comedian," I said.

"Naw! Say it ain't so, girl!" He gave me the most disappointed expression I'd ever seen on a man, and I'd seen a lot of disappointment during my time at the bookstore. It happened whenever I told book lovers their special orders wouldn't be arriving in time for the weekend.

"I'm only here to watch the open mike," I said.

The man kept shaking his head. "But you're so dang funny."

"What gave you that idea? I haven't said anything funny, unless you count my name, which, I suppose, is kind of funny."

He gave me a serious look, eyebrows raised. "But you *are* funny, aren't you?"

"I am pretty funny," I admitted nonchalantly.

He pointed at me. "I knew it. I have a special sense just by looking at people. I have the best eyes in the business."

"You should partner up with my friend Mitzy. She's always smelling people. The two of you could form a new talent agency. You could call it Scratch and Sniff."

Rather than laugh at my joke, the man gave me an appreciative nod, which I sensed meant more than a laugh. "Not bad. You can think on your feet. Keep working on it, girl. You're going places."

Just then, Mitchell emerged from the club and flashed his eyes at me. I had become fluent in Mitchell and knew his eyes were telling me to stop chatting with the doorman and come in already.

I ran up to my friend and hugged him. He looked like a new man in his new clothes.

"Nice look," I said in admiration. "The personal shopper really came through for you."

"I feel ridiculous," Mitchell said.

"You don't look ridiculous. Are those pants leather?"

"They are," he said, a sly grin curving up his mouth. Mitchell didn't feel as ridiculous as he'd claimed. "You should see my butt."

"Show me that butt," I said, and he did, shaking his adorable leather-clad tush as he led the way into the dark comedy club.

Chapter 15

I'd never been to a comedy show before.

I had seen plenty of comedy specials from the safety of my own living room, so I thought I knew what I was in for, but it was completely different.

When you're watching comedy at home, the comedian on the television can't see you. You've probably never given that a second thought.

But when you're sitting in an audience, live, the comedian can see you, hear you, and if their noses were as good as Mitzy's, even smell you.

I felt the pressure on us, the audience, growing with each performance.

The structure of the show was an open mic, with several venue regulars getting up to perform short sets in between newcomers and first-timers.

As one after another comedian came on stage to perform, the three and five minutes' worth of material could feel much, much longer. I could feel the performers on stage watching us, the audience, even more closely than we were watching them.

I found myself laughing at jokes just to be polite. I plastered a big smile on my face just in case one of them happened to be looking my way following a cringe-worthy punchline.

The other thing that was different about the live show compared to a filmed performance from a professional was... how would I put this kindly? The level of *polish*.

When you watch a comedy special on a streaming service, you're seeing a tight forty-five minutes of material that the comedian has honed to a glossy sheen. The material gets developed while the comedian performs the material on the road, over and over, in city after city, for a year or more.

What we were watching that night at the open mike was comedic material in its most raw form.

After the first dozen people had come and gone, and my expectations had been readjusted, I began to actually enjoy the show in all of its raw glory.

Soon I was laughing out of genuine mirth, not just politeness.

The performers' visible discomfort didn't take away from their efforts. If anything, by making comedy look hard instead of easy, I gained more appreciation for what they did. I felt their victory with them whenever they nailed a funny twist.

More people came and went, some of them objectively terrible. It didn't help that the worst ones spent their precious stage time muttering to themselves and blaming the audience for their lack of success.

Mitchell leaned over and said to me, "I'm so glad it's a good show tonight. Sometimes the open mike night can be a little rough."

This was better than average? I suddenly let out my biggest laugh of the night.

Luckily for me, my outburst happened around the time the visibly sweating comedian on stage was mangling what might have been a punchline. The comedian beamed directly at me, took a bow, and handed the microphone back to the MC.

The MC, a young man with a baby face and thinning hair, unfolded a piece of paper and announced, "Ladies and gentlemen—mostly the gentlemen—you're in for a real treat. There's an internationally famous underwear model in the audience tonight."

Heads spun around. People craned their necks to spot the model. I also turned to look behind me. It hadn't yet dawned on me that the MC was talking about yours truly. Mitchell must have known, because he began shaking with laughter.

"And I'm told she's funny, too," the MC said. "Our doorman knows how to spot talent, and he tipped me off. I honestly don't know who put her name in the hat for the open mike. It must have been her. I'd never stoop to such levels."

My cheeks flushed with heat. He was definitely talking about me.

The MC pulled up a stool and adopted a casual, it's-just-us-friends-here pose. "Usually, this is the point in the show where I tell you about our performers' various podcasts, and you folks, being smarter than me, get up to use the washroom. But how about we try something different tonight? How about we get the famous underwear model up here and see what she has to say?"

I covered my face with my hands, not that it would do any good. Where was a cloak of invisibility when you needed it?

"Aww, she's shy," the MC said. "Or is she just playing shy? What do you think? I mean, what kind of a shy girl takes off her clothes and poses for billboards in her underwear?"

The audience laughed.

"Wow," the MC said, pretending to nearly fall backward off the stool. "You guys can laugh, after all. When Badger and the Duck were up here, it got so quiet, I thought we'd had another gas leak and everyone was dead."

People laughed again, though not as loud.

"Let's keep the good times rolling," the MC said. "She's only five feet from the stage, and I know we can get her up here if everyone believes hard enough. So close your eyes, make a wish, pray to your gods, and when that doesn't work, make some noise until she gets up here."

People began making noise.

The MC stood, kicked back the stool, and roared, "Ladies and gentlemen, for the first time ever at this fine establishment, which does *not* have any current outstanding health violations, please welcome Peaches Monroe!"

I looked over at Mitchell.

He mouthed the words *I'm so sorry.*

I turned to Mitchell's husband, Byron, who was so mortified, he looked like he was about to lay an egg.

The audience was stamping their feet, clapping, and cheering for me to go up.

I got to my feet, stepped over the row of lights that was the only barricade between the stage and the audience, and wiped my palms on my hips.

The MC held the microphone away from his mouth and leaned in to say to me privately, "I didn't think you were going to come up here."

I asked, "What did you think was going to happen?"

He gave me an apologetic look. "Honestly, I was going to give you a hard time in between sets for as long as you could take it. Then I was going to make fun of you after you left."

"I'm getting the sense that comedy is a brutal business," I said.

"You're a quick learner," he said. "Good luck with your debut."

He pulled the microphone back to his mouth and said, grinning, "You asked for her, and you got her! Don't say I never give ya nothin'! Here for her debut performance, you saw her here first, Peaches Monroe!"

There was more applause, but not as boisterous as it had been a moment before. I sensed, using my completely new comedy-club senses, that the audience's short attention span was already drifting.

Someone yelled, "Take your clothes off!"

I leaned into the microphone and said, "That's not very polite."

The man yelled, "Please!"

I replied, "I will if you will."

The audience oohed in appreciation.

I shielded my eyes from the bright stage lights so I could see the guy who'd been heckling me. He stood up and began removing his shirt. He was wearing a tight-fitting T-shirt, and it wasn't coming off easily. I said the first thing that popped into my head.

"That's a cute shirt," I said. "Does it come in men's sizes?"

The audience laughed much louder than I would have expected them to, given it was such an obvious joke.

The man gave up on trying to remove his shirt again and sat back down. He waved for me to carry on.

I turned away from him and said, "Mr. Tiny Shirt gives us his permission to continue the show. Isn't that nice?"

The audience was silent. Of course they were. I hadn't said anything funny.

The lights shining on me were as hot as they were bright. My brain spiraled wildly, making connections. I mumbled something about my father disapproving of the wattage being wasted.

No response.

"If you knew my dad, you'd find that funny," I said.

Someone yelled out, "I'll be your daddy tonight!"

I gave the new heckler a dead serious look and said, "Sir, you don't have nearly enough chest hair for that."

The audience generously gave me some laughter. I felt myself soaring on the sound. I could do this! A new joke came to my brain and made its way to my lips. Before I could get it out, the MC was suddenly back on the stage, taking the microphone from my sweating hand.

"Nicely done," he said in my ear.

Into the microphone, he said, "Isn't she sweet, folks? That's our Peaches! As sweet as they get."

He subtly hip-checked me in the direction I was to take to exit the stage.

I left the heat and the lights and stepped into darkness.

The waitress who'd been serving us that night handed me a glass of ice water. "That was really fun to watch," she said. "How do you feel?"

Behind me, the MC was introducing the next open-miker. The words all ran together.

The waitress asked, "Are you okay?"

"I... I don't know. I can't feel my feet. I can't feel my legs."

She grinned. "It's the best feeling ever, isn't it? Greatest high on earth. It ought to be illegal. I got hooked five years ago."

"Are you a comedian, too?"

"We all are," the waitress said. "Everyone who works here, from the cooks to the valets. It's how we buy stage time."

"You buy stage time? What do I owe for... that?" I thumbed in the direction of the stage.

She laughed. "It's a figure of speech," she said. "I'm off the serving schedule tomorrow, so I'll be performing. It should be a good night. Sundays are surprisingly busy. Are you going to come by?"

A more rational person might have waited a minute before answering, but not me. I was still buzzing with adrenaline.

I replied, "What time do the doors open?"

Chapter 16

Saturday, April 8th

(One Month Later)

Dalton appeared in the doorway of my walk-in closet. He was wearing a sharp gray suit with a yellow tie. He leaned against the doorframe and adjusted his cufflinks, reminding me of a spy in an action-thriller movie. Funnily enough, the screenplay he'd been working on with Tyler in his free time was an action-thriller movie.

"You sure clean up good," I said as I wriggled into some jeans.

He watched me and said, "Are those jeans going on or coming off?"

I batted my eyelashes at him. "As much as I'd love to let you take them off, I'm afraid I don't have time to play. I have to get to the club and get some notes from the guys before my set." The club was the comedy club, and the "guys" were the group of aspiring comedians I'd befriended—as much as you could befriend a pack of scruffy animals such as them.

He frowned. "You're not going to the club tonight. It's the Zimmermanns' spring party. They'll be heartbroken if you don't make it."

"We talked about this," I said. "Did you forget to mark your calendar, DD? I've got momentum. People are coming regularly to see me perform. If I'm not there, I'll lose all my momentum."

His forehead wrinkled. "I remember talking about momentum, but not about you missing the Zimmermanns' spring party."

I slowly buttoned my jeans. Had I not talked to him about missing the party? I remembered *avoiding* talking to him about it, because I was waiting for the right time to break the news. Had the right time not come around?

"I hate to miss the party, but... momentum."

He made a disappointed sound. "I guess I'll go by myself."

"Why don't you bring Tyler? He'd love to schmooze with all those Hollywood people."

"I am bringing Tyler. He's getting dressed in the guest room right now."

"Then you don't need me," I said, frowning at the contents of my closet, pretending to have switched my focus entirely to picking out a shirt. The truth was, I knew exactly what shirt I was going to wear. It was one Mitchell had gotten custom-made for me. It read Team Peaches, and had ripe fruit on the front. The first secret of comedy was to make fun of yourself better and faster than the audience could.

"I don't like your new schedule," he said. "It seems like you're always in the city whenever I'm free." It didn't just seem that way. It was true.

I gave him what I hoped was a cute smile. "You're perfectly welcome to come in with me any night you're free. I'm only on stage for a few minutes at a time. Then I'll be right by your side the rest of the time."

Dalton wrinkled his nose. He appreciated my comedic stylings, but only on a one-on-one basis. He claimed to enjoy comedy, but objected to the club itself for aesthetic reasons.

"They've *really* cleaned up the club," I said, trying to sell it. "The rodent guy says the patches in the walls have held up. Rat-mageddon is behind us.

The best thing about Rat-mageddon is how good it looks in your rearview mirror."

Dalton wrinkled his nose even more.

"Yeah, I heard it, too. My bit about the rats is still pretty rough, but I'm working on it." I pulled out my notes and crossed out the page for Rat-mageddon. "I know there are a few good rat-based laughs in there, but I'm not there yet."

Dalton gave me the same blank, mildly confused response I got from audiences more often than not. My comedy was still at the stage where most of the laughs came from my fellow aspiring comedians, howling out of relief that it was me bombing on stage and not them.

Dalton said, "I'll tell John and Mitzy you came down with something."

"Don't lie on my behalf."

An unmistakable look of annoyance passed over his beautiful features. "I'm not lying on *your* behalf," he said coldly. "It's about protecting my career. What will they say if they find out I let you blow off their party just so you could jiggle around on stage for a bunch of drunk tourists and frat boys?"

"Um... you're *letting* me do that?"

He looked down. "You know what I mean." He met my gaze with earnestness. "I thought we were a team."

I sighed and began unbuttoning my jeans. "You're right," I said. "We are a team. I'll get ready for the party. It's a good thing I shaved my legs this morning. Which one of my cocktail dresses do you think looks good with your suit?"

He turned to the dresses and started sorting through them.

After less than thirty seconds, he let out an exasperated sound and stepped back.

"I'm not going to make you go," he said, looking down. "You should go to your comedy night. It's what you want to do."

"But I also want to make you happy," I said. "Plus the party sounds fun. I've never been to a garden party with a full big band." I started pawing through the dresses. The yellow one was a strong contender. "Of course I'm going."

"You're not going," Dalton said firmly.

I put my hands on my hips and stared up at him. "Do you want me to go to the party or not?"

"I want you *to want to* go."

I let out an exasperated breath. "Honestly, at this point, I don't care either way. Now I'm in a bad mood. You can uninvite me from the Zimmermanns' party if you want to punish me, but I'm just going to stay home and sulk."

"Suit yourself," he said lightly, and he walked away.

I sat down on the floor of the closet in a defeated pose.

I waited until I heard the garage door opening.

Then I jumped up, pulled on my trashy Team Peaches T-shirt, and ran to the bathroom to finish my stage makeup.

Chapter 17

My comedy momentum continued through April. Dalton forgave me for not attending the Zimmermanns' party, but he only came to see me perform once and declared that he was definitely allergic to something inside the club.

On the first of May, the comedy club closed for renovations.

That actually turned out to be a good thing.

My relationship with Dalton had been showing some cracks, but it turned out the removal of my preferred comedy venue was just the thing to get us back on track.

Every weeknight in May, I was at the house waiting for him every night when he got off work. He loved that.

We also spent every minute of the weekends together.

In fact, we were getting along so well that it was downright nauseating. Bernard did mention something about the increasing levels of sweetness in the house, and how he might be developing a toothache.

One Wednesday in the middle of May, Dalton surprised me in the morning by saying, "You should come to work with me today."

I sat up in bed. "Is it Bring Your Blonde to Work Day?"

He was getting dressed already. He smiled as he pulled a black designer T-shirt over his head. "Not exactly, but that does sound like a policy I could get behind."

"Why are you inviting me to come in today? Does your on-set assistant have the day off? Do I have to fill in by fetching you coffee and calling you DD?"

He laughed. "My assistant will be there. And you can call me anything you like, my princess." He leaned down and kissed me. "If you're coming, you do need to get up now."

I jumped out of bed. I'd been waiting over four months for an invitation to the set. I'd heard so many stories about it from Dalton, and I was dying to see if the sound stages looked the way I imagined.

As I rushed around getting dressed, he said, "I wouldn't have waited so long to bring you, except you explicitly told me you didn't want to be on set when I had a scene where I was shirtless and emotional, or if I would be kissing someone. It's funny, but this season has included more nudity than ever before."

"No kissing today?"

"Only with my favorite blonde, on breaks."

"That sounds hot," I said. "Can we make out in one of the rooms? I'd love to try one of the round beds with the satin sheets."

"Peaches, you do realize there are cameras and crew everywhere, don't you?"

"Everywhere?"

"I'm not really an ageless vampire, and those beds aren't nearly as comfortable as they look. They're not even beds. They're actually plywood, topped with a thin layer of foam. Actors can't move around much if we're sinking into a pillowtop."

"Way to ruin all my perfectly good fantasies."

He grinned. "We'll get you some new ones."

I finished getting ready, and we drove off together.

* * *

When we got to the studio, everyone who worked there was running around busily, talking frantically on headsets and barking orders at each other.

Dalton introduced me to a few people. They were polite, but I could see by the whites around their eyes that something was making them anxious. Was it me? Some of the crew had the jumpy demeanor of people who were expecting to get yelled at.

We got a moment alone, and I said to Dalton, "What's with your crew? Are they always this skittish? That skinny one on the ladder trembled visibly when I waved at him just now."

"They are jumpier than usual," he said, looking puzzled. "It might be because we're setting up some complicated shots today for the season finale. I bet that's it."

A short, middle-aged woman who'd been hovering near us leaned in and whispered, "It's because of that clueless grip that got fired last week for yawning. Everyone's been pounding double espressos because they don't dare yawn."

Dalton snapped his fingers. "That's it," he said. "I forgot about that because I was in the prosthetics department when it happened." He patted the woman's shoulder. "You're the best on-set assistant any actor could have." He turned to me. "Peaches, this is the mean lady who's always texting you the bad news about me working late."

"BB," I said, shaking her hand. BB was Dalton's nickname for the woman, whose name was Barbara. "It's so nice to finally put a face to the legend."

She stared at me as she shook my hand. "You're even prettier than your pictures." She turned to Dalton. "DD, why didn't you tell me she was even cuter in real life? And why haven't you brought her in before now?" She gave him a motherly slap on the wrist. "Shame on you, keeping this ray of sunshine away from us trolls in the dungeon."

Dalton gave me an eye roll and said, "BB has the most colorful way of expressing herself."

BB turned to me. "Have you had any coffee yet?"

I shook my head. "Your boy, DD, rushed me out of the house before I could grab any."

"Let's get you a cup before the yawns kick in. Being on set is mostly about waiting around. They call it *hurry up and wait*. It's like war. Boredom punctuated by bouts of extreme panic. It can wear a person out and cause yawning. Now, you technically can't be fired, since you don't work here, but we don't want to take any risks."

Dalton kissed me on the forehead. "I'm off to hair and makeup. BB will take care of you."

I made eye contact and gave him a double squint. He gave me a triple squint back. It was our secret way of communicating our feelings without being terribly mushy and giving bystanders a toothache. Sometimes we'd get all the way up to ten squints before stopping.

BB took me over to the craft services. She gave me a high-speed rundown on which snacks were better than they looked and which ones were to be avoided. I decided to take my chances with a large cup of yawn-preventing coffee and a jalapeno pretzel.

BB introduced me to a few other people, including the director. He seemed friendly enough, and not like someone who would fire a crew member just for yawning. Then again, what did I know? We were in Hollywood, after all, where people were often not what they seemed.

I found myself a bench in an area where people weren't measuring, lighting, or filming anything. I silenced my phone and settled in to watch the magic unfold.

The magic, as it turned out, unfolded at a snail's pace. *Hurry up and wait*, indeed.

There were, however, moments of brilliance, such as when Sir Drake Cheshire delivered one of his famous monologues. He did it flawlessly on the first take. It was all I could do to restrain myself from cheering for him. I'd been a dedicated fan of the show for years, whereas I'd only been Dalton's girlfriend for less than five months. The fangirl side of me was almost stronger than the girlfriend side.

As they were wrapping up for the day, BB came to see me.

"Scooch over," she said, and she joined me on the bench. "Have you actually been sitting on this hard thing all day? Your butt must be as sore as my feet," she said.

I nodded toward the center of the filming action. "I've been eyeballing that comfy chair over there, but something tells me it's got Director written across the back for a reason."

BB chuckled. "You catch on fast," she said. Then she turned and gave me a serious look. "How's he treating you?"

"The director? He hasn't tried to fire me, even though I must confess I did nod off for a while between two and three o'clock."

She gave me a motherly look. "Not the director. Dalton. Is he treating you well?"

"He's the best," I said.

"Have you had your first big fight yet?"

I had to think about it. "Maybe? There was a party I missed because I wanted to perform at a comedy club."

BB nodded sagely. "I heard about that."

"He did forgive me, and we made up."

BB didn't say anything.

"What?" I asked. "Is he still mad about that? What did he tell you?"

"He may have mentioned some concerns," she said, rapidly adding, "I'm sure it's only because he wants to protect you from the show business world. It can be treacherous."

"The other comedians I've been hanging out with are brutal," I said. "My skin is getting thicker every day. Plus I've already dealt with all the haters online."

"And how do you deal with that?"

"I don't go online," I said.

"Smart girl." She smiled. "I think you'll be just fine."

"Thanks."

"But..." She chewed her lower lip hesitantly. "Be careful about what you share in your act. Audiences are like locusts. They'll take everything if you let them. They're worse than Hollywood producers, and that's saying a lot."

"I'll take that under advisement. Do you want to come to an open mike sometime? You can give me —"

She cut me off with a laugh. "Not on your life," she said. "I'm with DD. I hate all comedy clubs."

I cocked my head to the side. "Dalton hates comedy clubs? I thought he just objected to the specific one I was going to, on account of the rats and whatever they use to clean the carpet that he's allergic to."

She got up from the bench and adjusted her clothes. "Did I say that? Honestly, I'm so tired today I don't know what I'm saying. I'd better get another coffee before I start yawning. Can I get you anything, sweetie?"

"I'm good," I said.

As Dalton's on-set assistant walked away, I thought about two things.

The first one was how motherly BB was. I'd imagined her as a twenty-something kid with stars in her eyes. Most of the other on-set assistants were very young, barely out of school. I found it interesting that Dalton, the orphan, had chosen a more maternal figure. Between BB and the dad-aged butler back at the house, Dalton had two parental figures looking after him.

The other thing I puzzled over was what BB had said about Dalton hating all comedy clubs. Was it true? He had wriggled his way out of going with me the first time I went. I'd assumed at the time that his writing meeting with Tyler had been spontaneous, but had it been?

And, if Dalton hated live comedy so much, when was he planning to tell me?

Chapter 18

"I get what you're saying, but BB is nothing like my mother," Dalton said.

He was driving, and we were on the way back to the house. I'd just told him about one of the observations I'd come up with after being on the set all day.

I replied, "I didn't say she was like *your* mother. Just that she's like *a* mother."

"What are you getting at? Do you think I'm a baby who needs looking after?" He shot me a grin to let me know he was only pretending to be offended. "Do you think that without BB taking care of me, I'd be completely off the rails, wallowing in tubs of cocaine?"

"Well... it does run in the family," I said, alluding to Josie. "But no. I don't think it's BB alone who has kept you on track the last few years. Bernard helps, too. BB is like a mom, and Bernard is like a dad."

"Don't tell him that," Dalton said with a chortle. "Ever since he turned fifty, he's gotten funny about his age. He's always accusing me of trying to give him a heart attack."

"He does that with you, too? I thought it was just me. The other day, I walked into the kitchen wearing a big sunhat, and the man shrieked in terror because he thought my hat was... honestly, I don't know what he thought my hat was. He's a great butler, but kind of a weird dude."

Dalton shot me another look. "But you like having him around, don't you? If you don't, I could see about hiring someone else if that would make you feel more comfortable."

"Don't you dare," I said. "He's a weird butler, but he's *our* weird butler." I reached over and squeezed Dalton's knee.

He smiled at the road ahead. "Traffic's not bad today," he said.

"That's good, because I forgot to use the washroom right before leaving the studio."

He made a tsk-tsk sound. "Number one rule of LA driving. Always use the restroom before you get in the car."

"I'm learning," I said.

He chuckled.

I carefully prepared to ask the question I really wanted a straight answer to. "Hey, speaking of me being a slow learner, the comedy club renovations are just about done. They'll be open this Friday, and I'll be doing some new material. Do you want to come with me, or... do you want to avoid it because you secretly hate all comedy clubs?"

I chewed my lower lip and waited for his response.

"I, uh, have a writing session with Tyler?" He phrased it as a question.

"Dalton, do you mean you have a session that you need to schedule as soon as we get home, so you don't have to go to the comedy club on Friday?"

He winced. "Yes." He winced again. "Don't hate me."

I didn't hate him. I was relieved he hadn't tried very hard to lie to me. That alone made it easier to forgive him for not telling me his true feelings about the club until now.

He asked, "What made you ask about that?"

"BB told me you hate live comedy," I said. "She didn't mean to, but she spilled the beans. Please don't be mad at her. She's a lovely woman."

"I'm sure she didn't mean to hurt your feelings," Dalton replied.

"Why would it hurt my feelings that you hate comedy clubs?"

"It's not that I hate them, exactly. I just... don't get it."

"What's not to get? You love it when I make you laugh. In fact, I'm already planning out my impression of Bernard being frightened by my hat. I'm going to do it for you tonight at dinner, and it's going to *kill*."

"That's different," he said. "I'm looking forward to seeing you do that."

"Then why can't you enjoy impressions by other people, at a cozy club that's completely free of vermin as of this month?"

He kept his eyes on the road ahead as he shrugged one shoulder. "Hard to say exactly. I'm an actor, so I fixate on the acting elements. Comedians are always sliding in and out of different characters. It's hard for me to stay with them. They're always doing the voice of some other person, then themselves, back and forth, except it's not really themselves, is it? They're playing a *version* of themselves, but they do it poorly, so you're supposed to know it's not *really* them. Nothing is real, but you're supposed to play along with the suspension of disbelief no matter how poor the acting is."

I stared at his profile. "You've put a lot of thought into this," I said. "Do you feel that way about my performances?"

"Of course not," he said. "But it's different. I *know* you. That's what makes it fun."

"If you came to the club regularly, you'd get to know the performers, and you'd feel exactly the same way. The better you know them, the funnier everything gets."

He didn't say anything.

"There's no rush for you to develop an appetite for comedy," I said. "This Friday, you can stay home and work on your screenplay with Tyler. That's fine with me."

"Is it really fine, or are you just saying it's fine to make me feel bad? Because it is working. I feel bad that I don't want to go."

"But not quite bad enough to actually go," I said.

He wrinkled his nose at the road ahead and didn't comment.

"Seriously, don't worry about it this time," I said. "My cousin Megan from back home will be down here, and she's already excited about going to the club. I'll have a full table of people cheering for me."

"Your cousin Megan? I knew she was coming to visit and drop off your bridesmaid dress, but is that this weekend? Wow. Time flies."

"She's coming *tomorrow*," I said. "She's coming Thursday and staying until Saturday or Sunday. You need to check your schedule more frequently, DD."

He grumbled in response.

Chapter 19

My cousin, Megan "Meenie" Gardenia, arrived on Thursday as planned.

She drove down with her long-time friend Rory, and Rory's guy, Duncan. I knew Duncan from the antiques shop he ran on Baker Street, but I didn't know him well. Rory and Duncan were on their way to Disneyland. They wouldn't be staying with me at the house—they were just dropping off Megan—but they did come in for a tour when they dropped off Megan.

After Rory and Duncan left, I said to Megan, "Now, *that* is a couple I did not see happening."

"Me, neither," Megan said, barely pausing to raise her eyebrows at me before going back to digging through my clothes. We were in my walk-in closet because she wanted to see if I had shoes that matched what she had in mind for her bridesmaids. She hadn't shown me the dress yet.

Megan was getting married June third, and so I planned on returning home shortly before that for a visit. By then, it would have been five months since I'd seen my family, which was the longest I'd ever been away from them, by a mile. I did miss them. I'd realized it the moment I'd seen my cousin. My eyes had suddenly filled with tears as the homesickness struck me out of the blue.

Megan, being the girl we'd nicknamed Meenie, had seen my tears and immediately gave me a hard time for being sentimental. Meenie was a special sort of girl. Her sense of humor was more of an acquired taste than my own. Lately, she'd been going by Megan, not Meenie, but I was free to continue calling my cousin whatever popped into my head at the time.

As she looked through my shoes, Megan explained the Rory-Duncan connection to me.

"It was all Rory's therapist's idea," Megan said. "Duncan is the crudest guy around—even cruder than me, if you can believe it—so the therapist felt that Rory hanging out with him was exposure therapy, as in exposure to all the things Rory freaks out about. Did you know she would run screaming from the room if someone said the word panties?"

"I did know about that," I said. "One time around Christmas, I was talking about my modeling in front of Tina and Rory, just casually describing the products, and it looked like Rory was going to pass out." Tina was also my cousin, and Megan's sister. Rory wasn't related to us by blood, but she had been Tina's best friend since they were kids, and most of us considered Rory part of the family.

"I still don't know if they're completely together or not," Megan said, frowning. "Rory refuses to discuss it, and Duncan, well, you can't believe anything he says."

"Hey, whatever happened to Duncan's stepmother? The former stripper who went by Cherry Pie?"

"She left town with her tail between her legs," Megan said. "Not that people cared that much about her stripping career. It was more the fact that she was a Grade A malignant narcissist."

"Ah, narcissists. I hear a lot about them since moving here."

"I bet you do." She pulled out a pair of silver heels. "These are perfect."

"Oh, darn. That means I won't have to buy new shoes."

Megan gave me a wide-eyed look. "You've changed," she said. "I don't remember you being interested in clothes. Not unless it was a corny T-shirt with a book-themed message, like *My Weekend is All Booked Up*." Megan pretended to gag.

I grabbed my cousin's hand and pulled her out of the closet. "You've seen my shoes. A deal's a deal. Show me this bridesmaid dress I've been hearing so much about."

We went to the bed, where the zippered garment bag lay.

I clasped my hands together. "This is it," I said, bouncing on my toes. "Since Nisha went and eloped on me, this may be my last chance to be a bridesmaid."

"Brace yourself," Megan said. She unzipped the bag.

I inhaled sharply.

The dress was perfect. It was like a gown that Cinderella might wear, but in a modern retelling of the fairy tale.

I started to say Megan had done well picking out a flattering style, but I couldn't get the words out because I'd burst into tears.

Megan snorted. "If you don't like the dress, just tell me." Clearly she was offended by my outburst. "If Malibu Barbie is too good for my wedding, just say the word, and I'll get someone else to fill in."

"It's not that," I said, struggling to get control over myself. "The dress is beautiful. I love it."

"Then why are you doing an impression of my Italian grandma at a funeral?"

"I don't know," I said.

"Are you upset about something else? Don't tell me. Is Dalton cheating on you with some on-set bimbo? I'll kill him for you. Just say the word." She punched her fist into her open palm.

"Nothing like that," I said. "I think... I might be... crying because... I'm happy?"

Megan rolled her eyes. Then, reluctantly, she gave me a hug.

I sobbed into her shoulder as it all came gushing out. I blubbered about how happy I was that she'd come to visit, and how I truly loved my life there, but I also felt torn, because I missed my old life back home.

"I don't even have a job anymore," I sobbed. "Riley is running the bookstore permanently. And she's better than me. Mr. Olivier says the sales are up five percent."

"Five percent is nothing," Megan said, patting my back. "Nobody can replace you, Peaches. You're irreplaceable. In fact, if you weren't coming back to be my bridesmaid, I was going to cut loose a groomsman."

"You're just saying that."

"Okay, I am," she said. "I could replace you in a heartbeat. But you are a very special person. You're my favorite cousin."

I sniffed. "You're the best cousin anyone could ever have."

"I know," she said. "Even better than Tina."

"Sure," I said.

I managed to pinch off my emotional outburst. I washed my face, removing my smeared makeup, then tried on the bridesmaid dress. It fit perfectly. I slipped on the shoes Megan had picked out and stood in front of a full-length mirror.

The shoes reminded me of Dorothy's in the Wizard of Oz. The shoes were red in the movie, but silver in the book.

"There's no place like home," I said, and I jokingly clicked my heels together.

"You look breathtaking," Megan said. "It's too good a dress to only be worn once. My future husband's family spent a fortune on it. Hey, I know! You should wear it tomorrow night at the comedy club. You could do a whole thing about being a bridesmaid. It would be really funny."

"But I don't have anything written about being a bridesmaid," I said.

Then something funny happened.

Even as I objected to the suggestion, ideas started popping into my head. One after another. All bridesmaid and wedding themed. There was nothing quite like declaring something to be impossible to get your brain working on proving you wrong. Brains were show-offs!

It all came together in my head.

I would wear the bridesmaid dress to perform on the following night, and I would, as the comedians say, *kill*.

Chapter 20

Friday, May 19th

Megan and I had a quick breakfast then drove into the city, where we met up with Dalton's half-sister, Josie Ranger, for shopping and lunch.

Megan and Josie hit it off, as I'd suspected they might.

The three of us went back to Josie's condo and hung out there to kill time until the comedy show that night. I'd brought my club outfit with me and planned it that way, since it didn't make sense to drive all the way back to the house just to turn around again and come back for the comedy show.

Josie had stopped into the comedy club and seen me perform a few times already. Unlike Dalton, she'd inherited the genes for appreciating live comedy. She'd worried it might be challenging to be around all the alcohol—she avoided bars for that reason—but the club served a pink soda with sugar-free grenadine that she enjoyed. Plus her issues had been more with hard drugs than alcohol. She could, in theory, have the odd drink, but she avoided it because drinking led to bad decisions about other things.

For dinner, we ordered sushi for delivery. We watched funny videos on Josie's big television as we ate.

I was nervous about my new material and wanted to try it out on the girls. They protested loudly and covered their ears. They wanted to experience it firsthand in the audience.

After dinner, I went to the washroom and practiced in front of the mirror with the fan and the taps running. I wasn't worried about the girls overhearing me. The white noise helped me relax.

I was working on my closer—the joke designed to get the biggest laughs at the end of the set—when I got a text message from Mitchell. He and Byron would be there, and they'd reserved a table in the front. There was space for all three of us girls, plus a couple of Byron's friends from work.

I'd never had so many close friends there at one time to watch me perform. I mentally crossed my fingers and hoped I hadn't bitten off more than I could chew. What was I about to do? I'd tossed out all of my reliable bits that had been working before the club's renovations and started fresh with all-new material about bridesmaids and weddings.

If comedy was about taking risks, I was going all in.

* * *

We got to the club, which looked and smelled better than ever. It was amazing what some paint could do. They'd also upgraded all the chairs and tables to a design that wasn't decades out of style. The previous chairs had been dotted with cigarette burns, which spoke of how ancient they were.

I seated my friends, introduced everyone to each other, then disappeared to hang out in the back hallway with the other comics.

The baby-faced MC came up to me and said, "You're getting ten minutes tonight, Peaches."

My jaw dropped. Ten minutes might not sound like much to the average person, but it was a lot for a new comedian. It was double the length of time most comedians performed on a late-night talk show.

"But I only have seven minutes," I said, panicking. I'd timed myself in Josie's bathroom, and even seven minutes would mean stretching it. "What should I do? Crowd work?" I wasn't that confident in my crowd work.

He shrugged. "Shake your peaches for all I care. As long as you keep them laughing and drinking." The MC was the owner's son, and he did love comedy, but he also kept cash flow in mind at all times. The other staff members complained about his obsession with beverage sales, but I didn't mind. I'd gotten some business experience running the bookstore, and I understood how things worked. It was one thing for people to come in and *appreciate* the books being there as a cultural thing, and another thing for them to actually buy stuff and support the shop.

I chatted with the usual guys and gals in the hallway about how I might stretch my material. They were in agreement that I didn't have to stick to the wedding premise for the whole ten minutes. The most important thing was that the jokes were funny. And even if they weren't funny, they had to at least sound like jokes. That would get me through a whole ten minutes with some dignity.

The woman who'd been waitressing on my first night in the club, Aquarius—actually her real name —said, "Whatever you do, don't go into storyteller mode. I know it's popular these days, and there are audiences that'll go along with it, but not here, and not from someone who's an unknown. Sorry. Real talk, girlfriend." She patted me on the shoulder and told me that, promising as I was, I was not a tenth as good as the five blond female comedians she rattled off next. Just hearing their names made my stomach clench. I'd never compare myself to those women.

Aquarius must have noticed the look of horror on my face.

She quickly said, "But you are better than some of them," and she rattled off the names of a few more blondes, some of whom had headlined at the club.

I beamed. "You really think so?" Genuine compliments in the hallway were as rare as hen's teeth.

"Nah," she said, laughing hard.

Aquarius had an infectious laugh, so I quickly joined in, which did make me feel better.

Then the other comedians started razzing me, sarcastically listing off the greatest comedians of all time who weren't as good as me.

Some people might characterize that behavior as bullying, but I'd learned to appreciate it as the twisted form of love it was. The other performers didn't razz people they didn't like or respect. Their sarcasm and playful taunts meant I was one of them. It also meant that, whether I stepped out on stage and ate crap for ten minutes or not, they'd still be there the next week, and so would I. We were in the trenches, but we were in it together.

All too soon, it was time for me to go on.

I stepped into the lights, and the MC made fun of my bridesmaid dress for a full minute. I was irritated with him until he leaned in and whispered, "That's one down, nine minutes to go." There were angels among us, and they took curious forms.

Once the microphone was in my hand, all my nervousness went away. I was focused and alert, but also completely calm. I was about to enter that rare state of mind artists call *flow*.

I opened by making fun of myself in the bridesmaid dress. People liked it.

Then I introduced my cousin as being there in the audience.

Heads craned, and there was confused murmuring. It was hard for the people sitting behind Megan to see her clearly, so that caused some confusion. The energy in the room ebbed in a way I didn't like.

Thinking fast, I brought them back with some salty language—not a staple for me, but effective when used sparingly.

They liked that.

They liked it so much that I found myself adding salty language to the rest of the jokes.

Everything flowed. I flowed with it. I was, as comedians like to say, *in the pocket*. I could have gone forever.

Out of the corner of my eye, I saw the flashing light that indicated I was one minute from the end of my set.

I paused and prepared to go all in with a long story about Cinderella, inspired by my dress. The imagined scenario started innocently enough, but then devolved into some rather graphic imagery involving a prince with a foot fetish doing terrible things to my glass slippers. It probably doesn't sound that funny when I describe it now, after the fact, but you had to be there.

The shoe-fetish punchline killed. What a closer! I'd never heard laughter like that—at least not when I'd been on stage.

I have no idea what happened next. The MC must have come on stage and repeated my name for more applause. Aliens might have landed and given us all examinations. What followed was about three minutes of my life that I have no recollection of.

The next thing I do remember was standing in the cool darkness at the side of the stage and getting hugged by Aquarius.

"You were so funny, girl," she said. "But I think you might be in big trouble. Real talk!"

"That's understandable. I slaughtered out there. Are Badger and the Duck ticked off about having to follow me?"

"Not them," she said. "Your boy is here. The actor."

"Dalton is here?" That couldn't be true. He was at the house, working on a screenplay with Tyler. He couldn't have been at the club.

"He's here, all right," she said. "And I don't think he liked your set. Not at all."

"What wouldn't he like about my set? It was perfect."

She gave me a wide-eyed *duh* look. "You made fun of him," she said. "A lot."

I pawed at the air. "Barely. For only a minute or two in the middle. And it wasn't anything intimate. It was just about how he didn't understand how wedding buffets worked because he'd only been to fake weddings on TV."

Aquarius shook her head. "He did not look thrilled." She backed away. "But what would I know? Men aren't my thing."

I thanked her for the information and went off in search of Dalton.

Chapter 21

I'd hoped that Aquarius had been wrong about my boyfriend being in the club, and his reaction to the material, but the woman was, as usual, spot on the money. Dalton Deangelo had been in the club, and he'd definitely seen my act.

When I found him, he was standing near the back with Tyler. As I walked up, he gave me a strange, awkward reaction. He stiffened, shoulders lifted and head sunk, like a wild animal trapped in a corner.

"Hey, babe," I said lightly. "Fancy meeting you here. Did you catch my act?"

"Yup. You did a whole nine minutes," Dalton said, smiling tightly. "Congratulations."

Tyler added in, "I timed you with my stopwatch. Like when you do your squats. I thought you'd like to know." Tyler was obsessed with using his stopwatch to time things.

"I know it was nine minutes," I said.

Dalton nodded. "That's longer than usual."

"It was," I said.

We all looked at each other. Nobody volunteered any comments on my act, let alone compliments. Tyler looked down at his stopwatch and started timing something. The awkward silence, perhaps?

After a moment, one of the other comedians came by on his way to the washroom, slowing down to slap my shoulder and say, "You killed up there, Peaches." He glanced at Dalton and Tyler and kept walking.

"Thanks," I called after his back. "I'm glad someone noticed."

I looked directly at Dalton. He took a sudden interest in Tyler's stopwatch.

"Yup," I said. "Here we are."

Tyler said to me, "You seemed like you were having fun up there."

My stomach lurched. That was never a good thing for a performer to hear. *At least you had fun* was the consolation prize for people who sucked.

I sensed that the red-haired personal trainer was being earnest, which made me even more frustrated by his backhanded remark.

"Fun is what it's all about," I said through clenched teeth.

Dalton swayed in the direction of the exit. "Well, we only popped in to catch your act and check out the renovations. We've still got a lot of work to do tonight."

Tyler said to Dalton, "We can stay for another..." He trailed off when he caught a look from Dalton.

"You guys should go work on your screenplay," I said flatly. "I'm sure it's of much higher caliber than anything you'll see in this grungy old hole."

Tyler looked around. "Grungy? I wouldn't say that. This place is actually not as bad as I remember."

"Be sure to write that down for the suggestion box," I said, pointing to the club's notorious suggestion box. It was rarely used by paying customers but always served as quality entertainment to the comedians, who abused it regularly.

I turned to Dalton, who'd never looked more uncomfortable—and I'd seen him having a full-scale meltdown at a charity function after an awful rumor about him went viral online.

The man looked like he was counting to ten inside his head, over and over, as he breathed in and out. I could almost see the numbers rolling across his eyes, like in a cartoon. I wondered to myself, would that make a good joke? *Counting breaths... counting sheep... counting cracks in the sidewalk... What was the funniest thing my neurotic actor boyfriend could count? What would make an audience laugh at him?* Those thoughts were not particularly helpful, but I was in comedy mode, and my wisecracking brain wouldn't shut off.

Tyler said, "Good work up there." He gave me a light punch on my arm. "I'll see you Tuesday for your workout."

"Maybe," I said. "Maybe not. You won't see me if I'm not around."

He gave me a confused look but said nothing.

Dalton brought his fist to his mouth and coughed three times. His fake allergies to the club had been activated.

He cleared his throat and said, "See you at home. Your cousin is staying with us for another night or two, right?"

"I don't know," I said, which wasn't true. Megan planned to stay the whole weekend then book a last-minute flight on Monday if she could get a deal. Her schedule was flexible.

"Well, whatever," Dalton said nonchalantly. "Have fun tonight with your friends."

"Josie's here," I said. "Did you even say hi to her?"

He wrinkled his nose. "Tell her I said hi." He leaned over and gave me a peck on my cheek. "Have fun tonight."

"Oh, I will," I said. "Fun is what it's all about."

He looked like he might say something but didn't.

Then he left with Tyler.

I was standing in the same spot, staring at the wall of famous performers' photos, when the comedian who'd complimented me on his way to the washroom, DeShon, emerged. He grinned as he wiped his wet hands on my arm and said, "Don't you hate it when you go all over your hands?"

I knew the dampness was only sink water, but I freaked out anyway.

"Easy, girl," DeShon said, wide-eyed. "Where'd your boyfriend go?"

I sighed.

He used the cuff of his shirt to dry off my arm. DeShon could be decent sometimes.

"He's got to go work on his precious screenplay," I said.

"Why?" DeShon grinned. "I've got three projects that would be perfect for him. Can he play a Latina woman? Or a green spider from outer space?"

I laughed. It felt good to have someone else making the jokes to cheer me up for a change. In my pre-comedy life, it had always been me trying to lighten everyone else's mood. I hadn't been on the other side much. I loved being around people who were as obsessed with keeping things light as I was.

"Dalton Deangelo can play any role," I said with authority. "He can even play the role of supportive boyfriend... but only to a point."

DeShon winced. "Ouch. Trouble in paradise?"

"I don't know. Maybe? This is uncharted territory. Are the girls you date supportive of your comedy?"

"No. Why would they? I make fun of them on stage, I'm never available in the evening, and I'm so broke that I borrow their deodorant."

"That does explain why you always smell so pretty, DeShon."

He looked past me at the stage. "I better get ready for my set. I've got a really tight four minutes. You and your friends are in for a treat."

"Then I'd better get seated with a drink in front of me so I'm ready."

DeShon winked at me. "Hang in there," he said.

"Why? Does it get easier?"

He shrugged. "How should I know?" He ran off with a bounce in his step.

Chapter 22

The next morning, I woke up with my face next to my cousin Megan's feet. We were in a bed together.

I sat up and stretched while Megan groaned about how hungover she was.

We were in Josie Ranger's condo, in the B-list actress's guest bedroom. All of us had enjoyed a very fun evening the night before, starting at the comedy club and progressing to a dance club. Mitchell and Byron and their friends had rounded out the group, making for a very enjoyable evening. I'd had so much fun, I hadn't even missed Dalton. And I'd had so many drinks, I hadn't been able to brood about his grumpy reaction to my act.

I was asking Megan how she'd gotten the big bruise on her shin when Josie, the sober one of the group, appeared in the doorway. She was wearing an apron and a comically large chef's hat. She held a large bowl.

"Good morning," I said. "Thanks for letting us crash here."

"I'm making bacon pancakes," she said excitedly. "That's where you pour a strip of batter over a cooked slice of bacon."

I jumped out of bed. "You had me at *bacon*," I said.

I joined her in the kitchen and helped her prepare a carbohydrate-heavy feast for the three of us. Like Dalton and most other celebrities, Josie only ate carbs on special occasions.

"Your cousin's pretty wild," Josie said. "Do you think she was serious about asking me to be a bridesmaid?"

Just then, Megan appeared, rubbing her eyes. "Dead serious," she said. "Josie, you have to come for my wedding. All my other bridesmaids are so boring."

I cleared my throat. "I'm right here," I said.

"I mean besides Peaches," Megan said. "How's she going to get into any trouble if she doesn't have a partner in crime?"

"She makes a good point," I said to Josie. "What's your schedule like?"

Josie blinked at us. "I'll have my people call your people."

Megan frowned.

"I'm free," Josie said, laughing. "I'm supposed to be on a panel for a comic book convention, but I can send my cardboard cutout. She's hotter than me, anyway."

I asked, "Why would you be at a comic book convention anyway?"

She gave me a mock offended look. "Uh, only because I'm the lead voice talent for the third-highest rated multiplayer online roleplaying universe, Goblin Online."

Megan and I gave her blank looks.

"It's a videogame," she explained.

I put my hand on my hips. "Why didn't you tell me? I demand to play this video game immediately."

"Me, too," Megan said.

Josie looked down shyly as she flipped the bacon-shaped pancakes on the griddle. "You two don't have to say that. It's just a dumb videogame."

"I'm great at video games," I said. "As long as someone points at the screen to let me know which car I'm racing."

"It's not that type of game," Megan said, and she explained a little about how it worked.

Megan and I were intrigued, so we ate breakfast and then started playing Goblin Online.

Five hours later, I checked my phone and saw that I had several text messages from Dalton. I didn't even open them.

Chapter 23

Megan and I quickly became obsessed with playing Goblin Online. I'd had no idea a videogame could be so much fun. I was used to being mocked by Adrian and teased by Noah about having no control over my avatar. This type of game, though, was so much easier for me to understand. Plus my goblin avatar was adorable, with her little potbelly and her spindly legs.

The three of us played all day Saturday then ordered sushi delivery for dinner again. Later, we returned to the comedy club to watch some of my more talented friends perform on the busiest night of the week. After that, we returned to Josie's apartment for another overnight stay. I took the sofa that time to avoid waking up with Megan's feet in my face.

Sunday morning, we went out for brunch at a trendy place that served all their drinks and meals on unusual dishes. I did not care for receiving a cappuccino served in a miniature porcelain toilet, but the waitress accommodated me by dumping it into a plant pot, which wasn't ideal, but I could live with it.

While we ate, some photographers came by and snapped pictures of us dining on the sunny patio. Josie removed her sunglasses and posed for the shots by pretending she didn't know the photographers were there. She was good at it.

My cousin was thrilled to be included. She gave the photographers her business card so they'd get the spelling of her name correct.

As the photographers left us to our brunch, Josie said to my cousin, "They probably won't run with your name, assuming you even get included in the shot. I'm not saying that to hurt your feelings. Just... don't get your hopes up. The sites that run the pictures know what sells. You'll probably get cropped out. I'm not sure Peaches will even make the cut." She gave me an apologetic look.

I pretended that it wouldn't bother me either way, but hearing that did bring my mood down. Nobody wants to be embarrassed online, but nobody wants to be left out, either.

Megan pouted. "I knew I should have stuck my face in between yours." She was sitting across the table from us, so inserting herself between us would have required some effort. She took a big slurp from her cappuccino mini-toilet. The beverage container hadn't bothered her one bit.

Josie asked, "Do you actually want to be semi-famous, Megs?" Josie called my cousin Megs, unlike anyone else, and Megan loved it.

Megan shrugged.

Josie said, "In that case, I could probably get you onto some sort of reality show. They're always looking for... interesting people."

Megan thought about it for a minute then said, "Nah. It's not the life for me. Peaches is way more interesting. I'm only here for a short vacation. I'll be heading home soon, getting married, and living vicariously through you two."

"It will be nice to head home," I said wistfully.

Josie ordered another round of cappuccinos, two flower pots and one mini-toilet.

Megan checked her phone and frowned. "So much for getting a cheap flight on Monday. It's not happening." She looked up at me. "You're going to be stuck with me for a few more days, cousin. Flying isn't going to work. I'll see if Rory and Duncan can make a detour on their way home. It's either that or a bus."

"You could drive up," Josie said. "Renting a car might not cost much more than flying."

Megan wrinkled her nose. "It's a long drive."

"I'll go with you, Megs," Josie said. She gasped and turned to me. "We could all drive up together," she said. "The three of us. We could take our time and have an amazing road trip."

Megan bounced up and down on her chair. "Does that mean you're going to be my bridesmaid?"

"Of course," Josie said. "If it's okay with Peaches."

"You can be my cousin's bridesmaid," I said. "As for me driving up..." I trailed off. Both of them looked so excited. I couldn't dash their hopes. "We can take my Mercedes," I said. "The old gal survived the last trip just fine, after all."

Both of them squealed then chattered away about what snacks we would bring on the road trip. Josie only snacked on unsweetened coconut chips, whereas Megan ate everything.

Our round of cappuccinos arrived.

Josie turned to me and said, "We should leave right now, in the next hour, and beat the traffic out of the city. We can take the I-5 and stop somewhere interesting, like Sacramento."

I asked, "How do we connect to the I-5 from the 101?"

Josie blinked at me. "What would we be doing on the 101?"

"I, uh, have to pack. And get Megan's things from the house."

"Except you don't," Megan said. "I only brought one suitcase with me, and it's at Josie's place." She looked me over. I was wearing the same casual outfit I'd worn during the day on Friday and Saturday. The only other clothes I had with me were the bridesmaid dress and silver shoes, which were in the trunk of Noah's Mercedes.

Josie also looked me over and said, "I could loan you some clothes. Bypassing the 101 would cut hours off our drive."

I had to laugh at the idea of wearing Josie's clothes. She wasn't just petite, she was downright tiny. Megan was much taller, and she was very strong from her workouts, but not much wider.

Megan said, "Peaches, didn't you leave town on New Year's Eve with nothing but your purse and a sequined cocktail dress? I know you did. I heard all about it."

I crossed my arms. "So?"

Megan gave me an exasperated look. "Peaches, all your clothes and things are still in your bedroom back home. You just have to make it there in those jeans. I've got some T-shirts that will fit you. And, besides, you can basically wear the same pair of jeans forever, so what's the problem?"

Both of them looked at me expectantly.

What was the problem?

I did have one big problem, which was leaving the state of California without even saying goodbye to Dalton. We hadn't spoken since I'd seen him at the club, though I had been in touch with Bernard to pass along the message I hadn't been kidnapped.

I also hadn't told my cousin or Dalton's half-sister about the trouble that had been brewing in paradise.

Would I tell them now and put a damper on their excitement about hitting the road immediately?

No. I wasn't the type of girl to rain on a parade.

I smiled at Megan. "Did you bring your I Love Beijing T-shirt? I'd wear that one."

Megan whooped with excitement. She had brought the offensive shirt. It read *I Heart BJ*, with the BJ being short for Beijing.

The other two began chanting, "Road trip! Road trip!"

Chapter 24

Friday, May 26th

(Four Days Later)

The sun was setting as I pulled up in front of the house I used to live in with Nisha. It looked smaller than I remembered. There weren't any landscaping lights that flickered on at dusk to light it up.

Josie was in the passenger seat next to me. The two of us were on our own, and had been for only twenty minutes. After three days together in the city plus four days on the road together, we'd just dropped off Megan, whom I'd also started calling Megs, at her place.

I turned off the car's engine. I was too tired from the road to get out of the vehicle, so I sat there. Josie must have felt the same way because she didn't move, either.

"Cute house," she said.

"It's a rental," I said.

"It's still cute." She turned her head. "Hey, there's the tree I hid behind to take your picture about a million years ago."

"There it is," I said.

Another minute passed.

The engine of the Mercedes made some settling-down ticking noises.

Josie said, "The car is so quiet without Megan. It's eerie." She looked over at me. "Is it weird that I miss her already?"

"It's not that weird," I said. "We've spent basically every minute together for the last seven days. If you didn't qualify as a close enough friend of

Megan's to be a bridesmaid before, you certainly do now."

Petite Josie furrowed her petite brow. "I'm nervous about meeting Tina and the rest of the family."

"Don't be," I said. "They'll love you like a sister, just like I do."

"Speaking of sisters and brothers, what's going on with you and Dalton? He sent me a few text messages asking the strangest questions, like what kind of mood you were in, how you were driving, and whether or not you were taking any prescription medications."

"That joker," I said. "He's probably just bored, trying to stir up trouble."

"Peaches," she said solemnly. "I didn't want to say anything in front of Megan, but I know my half-brother well enough to tell when he's stirring up trouble versus when he's legitimately concerned about something. Did you two have a fight?"

"Yes," I said, then, "No. I don't know. Remember how he was acting at the comedy club last week?"

"He was at the club?"

I pointed at her. "Right. I didn't tell you. Dalton said to say hi that night, by the way. *Hi*. Please mentally backdate that by seven days." I shook my head. "He might have told you himself except he couldn't get out of there fast enough."

She wrinkled her nose. "He didn't like you mentioning him in your act, did he?"

"I suspect he did not. Either that or he didn't approve of my salty language. Or all of the above. I don't know because he won't tell me. I called him from the road, several times, and he took my calls, but he didn't want to talk about what happened that night at the club." I shivered and rubbed my forearms. Without the car heaters running, I was getting a chill. It was nine o'clock at night, and even though it was May, the weather wasn't nearly as nice as back in California. I'd almost forgotten my arms could get goosebumps.

"He won't talk about it," Josie repeated, nodding. "That sounds like what happened between you and your previous boyfriend. You two and all your drama."

I nodded. She had heard the entire saga of Peaches and Adrian. On our second day in Sacramento, I'd told her and Megan about how I'd had a baby with Adrian. Megan had been blown away by the secret. Nobody in the family had suspected. She asked who else knew, and I told her I'd checked with my parents and Elliot, and that we were gradually telling people, one at a time. She was free to tell her sister and mom.

We'd spent half a day discussing childbirth. It made me feel even closer to both of them that they knew the truth.

Josie said, "I'm glad I know about Elliot, because otherwise the whole situation with Adrian would look a lot worse. You two and all your... codependent entanglement."

"My entanglement?" I snorted. "It's mild compared to your family. Let's not forget that your half-brother had an affair with your *other* half-brother's mother."

A look of hurt crossed her delicate features.

"Sorry," I said. "I didn't mean to make it sound so... scandalous."

She smiled. "It's okay. I'm the first one to admit how scandalous my family is." She glanced over at the house. "Should we head in and hunker down for the night? Megan's not with us, so we can go to bed nice and early for a change."

I checked that I still had my house key—I did—and we got out of the car.

The house was eerily dark. Nisha and Noah had already left for their cross-country adventure and wouldn't be back in time for Megan's wedding. I wasn't paying rent at the house anymore—Noah had taken over my share—but they'd both given me express permission to stay for the week leading up to the wedding. All my stuff was still in my old bedroom, anyway. It would give me a chance to pack. Assuming I even wanted to pack. Maybe I'd settle into my old routine and not want to go back to California, and a future of fighting with Dalton about my comedy aspirations.

I opened the front door. It let out a familiar squeak. Then a familiar scent wafted out. It was the particular scent of the old house, mixed with Nisha's incense and scented candles. I hadn't realized how much I'd missed the smell of the house until that moment.

I choked back some unexpected emotion and put a smile on my face.

"There's no place like home," I said, waving Josie in ahead of me.

Chapter 25

Sunday, May 28th

(Two Days Later)

"She's so young," my mother said, referring to Josie.

The two of us were washing up after dinner. Josie Ranger was still at the table, playing a board game with my father and Elliot.

My mother asked, "How old is she?"

"Twenty-eight," I said. "She only told you twice over dinner when you asked, Mrs. Nosypants."

My mother hip-checked me out of the way playfully and took over at the sink. "That's what she told me, but we all know how Hollywood people fib about their age."

"We do?" I smirked as I grabbed the tea towel and began drying.

"I can't say I blame them," she said, sniffing lightly. "If I could make a few years go away, I would do the exact same thing."

"Not this again," I said. "Are you still feeling sorry for yourself about getting older?"

She shot me a dirty look. "It's real," she said. "I'm not imagining it."

"Sorry," I said immediately, changing my tone. "Is there something going on that I don't know about?"

"Besides my daughter abandoning me without any notice? Not much. Except I *am* in withdrawal from a powerful drug."

I knew about the first part, but not the second. My mother wasn't the type to do drugs, unless you counted Oreo cookies, which everyone knows are basically drugs.

I asked, "What are you talking about?"

She gave me a dead-serious look. "The drug is estrogen. I'm in withdrawal right now because my body decided to stop making it. My estrogen-factory ovaries have shut down."

"You mean menopause? Are you sure? Did the doctors test your hormones?"

She gave me a *duh* look. "I know my own body, Peachy. I'm five months into my change year."

"I had no idea," I said.

"At first, when I missed a month, I thought it was just anxiety about you being all the way down in California. You should have seen me. I was a total stress ball. My shoulders were up around my ears. Nothing could make them come down. I saw a massage therapist, who didn't know what to make of it. It was awful. Not only was I stiff as a board, but I couldn't stay asleep at night, I couldn't stay alert during the day, and my heart would just start racing for no reason at all."

"Mom," I said, my throat aching. "Why didn't you tell me?"

She waved a hand. "Nobody wants to hear about some old lady's problems. Besides, everyone goes through it. My mother did, and every woman before her. Did you know Astrid went through the change of life two years ago? Of course, being Astrid, she only had three hot flashes over a couple of days and then it was done." My mother made a sour face.

"It's my fault," I said, feeling guilty. "If it happened right after I left, it must have been me. I triggered it." I looked down at the platter I was drying. I got a flash from my memory. I had been drying that platter with Adrian on that first family dinner after he'd arrived back in town. I shook my head and tried not to think about him. I was already feeling bad enough about abandoning my mother when she needed me.

"Don't blame yourself," my mother said. "It's probably for the best you're off living your own life, hanging around with young movie stars and doing your comedy nights with all the young, famous comedians. I'm sure it's quite fun. Your father and I enjoy watching the comedy specials on TV, you know."

"Mom," I said. "Are you okay? Really?"

She stopped washing dishes and rested her forehead on her hand. "I'm just tired," she said weakly. "So tired."

I grabbed her by the shoulders and steered her over to the stools.

"You relax," I said. "Let me finish the dishes."

Without looking up, she said, "I'm not really in the mood for entertaining. Do you think your friend Josie would mind if I went straight to bed?"

"She'll understand," I said. "Are you sure you're okay?"

She looked up, her blue eyes tinged with red. Her voice hoarse, she said, "What if it's not menopause? What if there's something really wrong with me?"

I tried to think of something reassuring to say. She'd comforted me so many times. What was it she'd always done whenever I'd come to her with my problems?

It came to me in a flash.

I hugged her and rubbed her back. Her muscles really were tense. "It's okay," I said. "Everything's going to be okay."

I felt her relax ever so slightly.

Chapter 26

When we got back to Nisha's house that night, I explained to Josie why my mother hadn't joined in on our second board game.

We were sitting in the living room with the television tuned to a channel showing vintage sitcoms.

Josie's face twitched. "My mother's going through it, too. That's strange how she described it. I never thought of it as a type of drug withdrawal. People say that all the time, about things like caffeine or sugar, but only because they've never had a *real* addiction."

Her words made me feel defensive on behalf of my mother. It was like when you pour your heart out about something and someone else points out that *some people have* real *problems*.

"Estrogen is technically a steroid," I said. "Like testosterone, except..." I trailed off. I'd read some pages of the book my mother had shown me, but the concepts had flown over my head and disappeared. I wasn't too worried. I had another couple of decades to go until it happened to me.

Josie stared at me blankly. She was probably thinking about her own addiction, which was more real to her than anyone else's could ever be. Not that anyone's life struggles could be compared to anyone else's. And maybe she wasn't thinking my mother was an idiot. Maybe it was just me, feeling defensive out of daughterly guilt.

I shrugged. "It's probably different for everyone," I said. "Bodies are weird."

Josie relaxed a little, sinking into the soft couch. She let out a light laugh. Hollowly, she said. "My mom probably isn't even there yet. If I know her, she's only using it as an excuse to act like a monster. She's supposedly been going through it for the last ten years." Josie looked away. She didn't like talking about her mother.

The television volume blared as the sitcom theme song came on.

Josie gave the screen a startled look then got to her feet. "If it's all the same to you, I'm going to hit the hay." She stretched and yawned.

I grinned. "I won't tell my cousin you went to bed before ten like an old lady."

Josie gave me an eyeroll and headed off for bed.

Josie was sleeping in my old room, surrounded by my old stuff. I was staying in Nisha's room, surrounded by all her world culture artifacts and scented candles. It had been Nisha's idea for me to stay in her room, since Josie didn't know my former roommate and therefore might be more comfortable around my stuff. Nisha was such a thoughtful, empathic person. I missed her so much. Being in her house and knowing she wasn't about to bound in the front door at any minute made me sad—or at least it would have if I'd dwelled on it.

I got up, tidied the living room, and went to bed myself.

* * *

When I woke up Monday morning, the house was very quiet.

I'd slept in late, but Josie was an early riser, so she should have been bustling around already.

I got up and checked my old bedroom. The bed was neatly made, and Josie's suitcase was gone.

I went to the kitchen, where I found a note:

Peaches, I am so sorry, but I have to get home. I'm on an early flight. Thank you so much for the amazing road trip. Love, Josie.

She'd signed it off with a cartoon drawing of a goblin, representing the video game character she voiced.

I immediately called Dalton. It was only the third time I'd spoken to him in a week.

"Hey, gorgeous," he said cheerfully. "You caught me at the perfect time. I'm in the makeup chair, getting latex glued to my face for a flashback scene. Everyone loved the season with Frankenstein's monster so much that we're going back to the ol' Fanservice Well for more. May the Fanservice Well never run dry!"

"Am I on speakerphone?"

There was a rustling sound. "Not anymore," he said. "What's up?"

"I need to talk to you about something."

There was a long pause, then, "The thing about that night at the club is... I had a lot on my mind. Plus Tyler was there. Can't we talk about this when you get home?"

"Sure. Fine," I said quickly. "I actually wanted to talk to you about Josie." I explained how she'd disappeared on me that morning without any warning. I read the note to him and asked what he thought.

"Yikes," he said. I heard him suck air between his teeth. "I'm sorry she bailed on your cousin's wedding, but that's Josie for you. She's not the most reliable person, in case you hadn't noticed. She's always running off on some new adventure without checking with anyone else."

I felt the hackles go up on the back of my neck. Was he talking about Josie, or about me? His comments did seem rather pointed.

I heard the makeup artist instructing him to switch the phone to the other ear.

There was a rustling, then Dalton said, "Are you still there?"

"I am," I said. "The reason I wanted to talk to you about Josie is... what if she's not on a flight right now? What if she's off doing drugs somewhere?"

"I hope she isn't," Dalton said. "But she is an adult. She's thirty-one."

I noted that thirty-one was three years older than the age she told people she was. My mother had been right after all. The woman had picked up some wisdom with her many years.

That gave me another thought. If Josie had lied to me about her age, what else was she lying about? Was she really clean, or had she been using drugs the entire last week? I hadn't been with her every minute, and she had taken an interest in some seedy-looking guys along the way.

I heard the special effects artist asking Dalton how long he'd be on the phone.

"Give me another minute," he said to her. To me, he said, "Can I call you back later? I don't mean to brush you off. It sounds like you're really worried about Josie. I could make some calls to a few of her other friends and check in on her."

"No need," I said. "Maybe the road trip was too stimulating for her and she was feeling tempted."

"I can only imagine," he said, sounding empathetic.

I took a big breath. "In which case, I have to give her credit. She probably made the right decision to get back home again and get back into her support system." I paused to swallow down the bad taste in my mouth. "I suppose the trip and Megan's wedding weren't the support she needed."

"There's no need for you to feel bad about not being enough for her, Peaches. My sister had problems long before you came into the picture."

How had he known exactly what I'd been feeling? Like my mother, the guy could be sharp about certain things.

"Thanks. I should let you get back to your special effects. I'll have to get busy finding someone else to fit the new bridesmaid dress my cousin ordered. Do you think Garnet's other sister enjoys bridesmaid duties?"

"Uh..." Dalton said.

"Her name is Perry," I said. "I think you met her. She does textile art. The scary puppets."

"It's not that," he said. "Listen, I'm not sure I can make it to your cousin's wedding on Saturday. Tyler got us a pitch meeting with some movie execs, and it's kind of a big deal."

"Ha ha. Very funny."

"I'm... not joking," he said.

"You're the famous actor, Dalton. Since when is a redheaded personal trainer lining up big-deal movie-pitch opportunities for *you*?"

He replied in a prickly tone. "Now is not the time to discuss this," he said.

I felt his irritation flowing over the phone line. It curdled my stomach, but was not unfamiliar. The last few conversations with Dalton had also taken a similar turn.

I replied in an equally prickly tone. "It's never a good time for you to discuss the things I want to discuss."

There was a long silence.

"I have to go," he snapped, and the call ended.

I dropped the phone on the kitchen table and stared at it.

Why was he so grumpy toward me over the phone? I didn't get it. Now, some women actually enjoyed the challenge of taming a grumpy man. I was not one of those women. And besides, he'd started out charming. This cranky side had only come out after I'd been living with him—living *for* him—at his beck and call for the last five months.

Had I spoiled him?

Or, like his half-sister, Josie, did Dalton have a lot more going on internally than what he was sharing with me?

Was keeping secrets something they had both inherited from their unabashedly narcissistic father, Jocko Ranger?

And was there something wrong with me that I didn't notice when other people were going through something?

I hadn't noticed Nisha falling in love with Noah.

I hadn't noticed my mother going through a big life change.

I hadn't... noticed I was pregnant until I was giving birth.

I wasn't the most observant person, was I?

Chapter 27

Tuesday, May 30th

Josie did send me a few messages to let me know she had made it home and was feeling much better. She asked what she could do to make it up to Megan for missing the wedding, and I assured her that my cousin would be understanding, which she was.

It turned out that the seamstress who was making Megan's bridesmaids' dresses hadn't yet cut a single yard of fabric for Josie's dress, so it was no problem to cancel the order.

Megan fluffed the colorful bouquet she was working on and said, "I just hope she's going to be okay."

We were standing inside Gardenia Flowers, the family business Megan owned and ran with her sister.

"She'll be so relieved you're not planning to fly down to LA and wrestle her into submission."

Megan gave me a catty smile. "It's her loss, anyway. At the ripe old age of thirty-one, this may have been her last chance to be a bridesmaid." I'd shared Josie's real age with Megan, and now I regretted it.

I snorted at my cousin. "And how old are you, exactly?"

The smile fell off her face. "I'm the one getting married, so being a bridesmaid is no longer a concern. From now on, I'm only up for Maid of Honor duties. Keep that in mind when you and Mr. Hollywood tie the knot." The grin came back again. "I'd like to make a dramatic entrance, by the way. How do you feel about the wedding party being dropped from an airplane?"

I shrugged. "As long as we have parachutes, that's fine by me." I leaned on the counter and sniffed some nearby roses. "Of course it's easy for me to make promises, seeing as how I'm never getting married, let alone to someone who can afford to parachute in an entire wedding party."

"Trouble in paradise?"

I bolted upright and crossed my arms. "Why does everyone keep saying that? Is it because Dalton lives in Malibu? Is it the name *Malibu* that makes people want to mock us and our problems? Everyone back at the club was always—"

Megan grabbed a nearby water bottle and spritzed me. "Calm down," she said.

I managed to calm down.

Megan shook her head. "And people say *I'm* the excitable one in the family."

"If you must know, there *is* trouble brewing in paradise," I admitted. "Dalton's not coming to your wedding Saturday. I'll be dateless."

Megan took it in stride, not even stopping before moving on to her next floral arrangement. The flowers were for a local wedding happening the next day. It was a lunchtime wedding for a sweet couple in their eighties.

"Maybe it's for the best that he's not coming," Megan said. "Without him around to distract you, you can take on more bridesmaid duties. I could use the help. Tina is useless. I blame Luca for getting her double pregnant. She's as big as a house and cranky as a bear." She paused, a look of horror dawning on her face. "What if she gives birth during the ceremony? It would be just like Tina to make everything about her. She loves attention."

I let the comment about Tina seeking attention pass. I didn't have a sister, but I'd observed enough sibling rivalry in other families to know better than to defend one sibling's mental image of the other sibling.

"Don't worry about Tina dropping her foals at your wedding," I said, lifting up my chin. "If there's any sign of waters breaking or contractions happening, I'll swing into action. I'll rip off the top layer of my skirt, catch the little todgers, one and two, then wrap 'em up like baby burritos. The rest of the wedding party can carry on as though nothing happened."

"Okay," Megan said, as though I'd said something reasonable.

We talked for another hour, finalizing arrangements for the weekend, and then I left her to the floral job.

I stepped out onto Baker Street, which felt incredibly familiar and yet strangely alien at the same time. There had been just enough changes to be unsettling. Not one or two but *three* businesses on the street had changed in the last five months.

A second wine store had popped up, one of the chiropractic clinics had become an insurance agency, and there was a taco restaurant inside a purple brick building that had once been home to... I had no idea. What*had* been there before?

Not being able to remember bothered me so much that I went inside and asked.

The employee working the front counter frowned at me. "What was here *last year*? You must be thinking of a different place. This has always been a taco shop." She pointed to the walls, which were filled with framed menus that had all been colored by customers. "We've been here for over thirty years," she said.

I backed away slowly, apologizing to the confused woman as I did.

How had there been a taco shop on Baker Street for thirty years? How had I never noticed?

I stepped out into the sunshine once more. I felt like the dumbest person on earth.

I glanced in the direction of Bookworm Books. I'd planned to pop in and check on Riley, but just thinking about seeing someone doing my old job made my stomach roll. I could only handle so much feeling stupid.

Keeping my head down so Riley wouldn't notice me, I marched past the bookstore and on to Donut Joe's.

Seeing Rhonda would cheer me up. Rhonda always knew how to make me laugh. She'd be delighted to hear more about my adventures with Dalton. She'd always been rooting for us, in her own way.

I walked into Donut Joe's.

The scent of vanilla and fried dough did a few things to me.

One, I immediately felt at home.

Two, my mouth began to water.

Three, I thought about how much my personal trainer would disapprove of me being there.

Now that was a new feeling. For the first time in my life, I'd felt personal-trainer guilt. Who knew that day would come?

I went to the counter. I didn't see Rhonda, so I ordered my usual and asked the young man working there if it was her day off.

He gave me a cagey look. "Uhh," he said. "Rhonda?" He looked around.

"Don't tell me," I said. "She's taking her break in the alley?"

He leaned forward, eyes wide. "Are you a friend of Rhonda's, or a customer?"

"I'm both," I said. "No. I'm a friend first, a customer second."

He struggled visibly as he said, "I'm sorry to inform you that Rhonda died."

I didn't comprehend his words. "Is she taking some time off? She did say something about getting up to the lake when the weather got warm. She's probably there."

The young man looked around then came out from around the counter to stand beside me. He tentatively put his sweaty hand on my elbow.

"I'm sorry," he said again. "Rhonda passed away."

He couldn't have been saying the words he was saying.

Rhonda couldn't be gone. Not permanently. Rhonda was probably up at the lake. The kid had to be mistaken.

He still had his hand on my elbow, and now he was saying something else, but it was just noise.

The donut shop was getting dark.

My mouth filled with saliva.

All the light around me narrowed to a pinprick.

Chapter 28

Thursday, June 1st

(Three Days Later)

The gray-haired woman working at the animal shelter cocked her head and said, "You look so familiar."

Ordinarily, I might have casually mentioned that I'd done a little modeling, but I wasn't in the mood. I hadn't been in anything resembling a good mood for a couple of days.

She went on. "I know you from something. Are you on the news? I know! You're the weather girl who substitutes for Lance Philby."

"I'm not the weather girl," I said. "Maybe I just have one of those faces that seems familiar."

The gray-haired woman looked me over from head to toe. "You look like that girl who does the underwear modeling. The bigger one with the real body."

I winced internally. All bodies were *real*, but I got the gist of what she was saying.

"You must mean Peaches Monroe," I said.

"That's it!" She snapped her fingers. "That's her name. You look just like her."

"Thanks," I said. "Does that mean I get a discount on adopting a cat or dog?"

She gave me a serious look and flatly replied, "The adoption fees are not negotiable."

"Fair enough," I said, then waved for her to lead the way.

She took me on a tour through the animal cages. I'd expected my visit to the animal shelter to be a heartbreaking errand, but to my relief, the cages were clean, spacious, and largely empty.

The woman asked over her shoulder, "Are you looking for anything in particular?"

"A cat," I said. "Female. Black and white, with a sort of white mustache."

"Excellent," the woman said, not slowing down. "I love it when people are specific. It makes my job easier. What about this one? I suppose you could call her muzzle markings a mustache." She stopped by a cage containing a sleeping black-and-white cat.

I put my fingers through the bars of the cage. The cat rose from her bed and came over to rub her chin on my knuckles in a friendly yet not desperate manner. I liked her immediately.

"I'll take this one," I said.

"Hmm," the woman said. "Are you sure you don't want to look around? This is one of the older females we have on hand. Most people would prefer to take on a younger animal with fewer health problems."

I kept petting the cat. "Does this one have any serious issues I should know about?"

The woman checked the notes on the door of the cage. "Nothing serious. She's missing a fang, but that shouldn't be an issue, unless you're bothered by a crooked smile."

"Nobody's perfect," I said with a shrug.

The woman gave me a smile that let me know she had forgiven me for my joke about getting a discount and could now see that I would be a responsible pet parent. She opened the door of the cage so I could get better acquainted.

The cat walked her front paws up my side. Suddenly, some sort of cat instinct I didn't know I had kicked in. I looped my arm under her backside as she leapt into my arms. I held her while she purred and rubbed her whiskers on my cheek.

The gray-haired woman looked surprised. "I've never seen a faster match. How is this happening? This can't be real."

"That's the thing about chemistry," I said. "You can't fake it."

The woman tilted her head. "But... how did you know?" She glanced around, as though looking for hidden cameras.

"Just a guess," I said, then, "Can I take her home now?"

"There's some paperwork to do. It won't take long. Right this way."

I turned to put the cat into the cage, but the affectionate feline refused to let go of me, so I took her with me.

We filled out the adoption paperwork. I paid the fee and added an extra donation for the shelter, then left with my new cat. My new *older* cat.

She meowed a few times on the drive home, but when I stuck my fingers into her cage she calmed down.

We got to Nisha's house, where I left her inside, in the crate, while I unloaded the rest of the cat stuff from the car. When I returned, she gave me a loud meow to let me know how she felt about being inside the crate. She pawed at the metal door.

I took the crate into the smallest room of the house—the bathroom—closed the door, and let her out.

She immediately went to the bathroom door and pawed it.

"I'm supposed to keep you confined to one room," I said. "We're supposed to take it slow and let you get your bearings. You heard the nice lady at the pet shelter."

The black cat with the white mustache gave me a you-can't-be-serious look.

I knew when I'd been beat. I opened the door and let her out.

She stepped out and strutted down the hall, her white-tipped tail held high.

I trailed behind like some sort of cat butler while she systematically inspected every room of the house before settling on a chair in the living room, where she began licking her paws.

I took a seat on the couch.

"I'm sorry you were at the shelter so long," I said.

She watched me with one eye while she continued taking her bath.

"Rhonda didn't have a lot of family, and her friends weren't able to take you in. I guess they thought someone would come along to adopt you eventually."

The cat continued bathing herself.

"They were right," I said. "As soon as I heard that your mama had passed away and left you behind, I knew that I could do something to honor her memory. Rhonda was a good woman."

The cat's ears twitched at the mention of her mama's name.

She jumped off the chair, darted across the living room, and jumped onto my lap.

"I miss her, too," I said.

Rhonda's cat settled into my lap. She stretched her back leg up, propping it against my chest, and noisily licked between her toes.

Chapter 29

By Friday, my life was better.

I still had a few issues. I was upset about Dalton bailing on the wedding. I kept worrying about whether or not Josie was truly as "okay" as she'd claimed to be in her recent text messages. And I felt anxious about my mother's transition into what she'd been jokingly referring to as "cronehood." (Not the most flattering term.)

But I said my life was better, and believe me, it was.

Friday morning started with the companionship of a very affectionate black-and-white cat. Rhonda's cat seemed to have been watching me sleep. When my eyes opened, she was staring into them. She stood, stretched, and came over to lick my face with her raspy tongue.

I haven't mentioned the cat's name because she didn't have one. According to the young man working at Donut Joe's, Rhonda had only ever referred to the feline as "my cat."

The animal shelter usually gave anonymous pets names, to help potential adopters connect with them, but they'd forgotten about the black-and-white girl. Or at least that was what I told myself, since the name they'd given her wasn't much of a name. The card on her cage had read Tuxedo Cat. I was considering going with Tuxedo, or Tux for short, but hadn't decided yet. I was still trying it out.

I walked into the kitchen and found my new roommate somewhere she wasn't supposed to be. Sitting in the kitchen sink.

"Tux, get off the counter right now," I said.

She continued to lick the water that dripped from the kitchen tap.

"That worked well," I said with snort. "It must be the name," I concluded.

She gave me an innocent look.

I walked over and wiped the water droplets from the top of her head.

"Tux is cute enough, but you don't know it's you, do you?"

The cat didn't respond, except to continue looking adorable.

Now, those of you who have cats will have noticed my complete absence of cat knowledge. I, however, still believed that the black-and-white cat would eventually respond to my verbal commands... once I'd found the right name.

"Well, I'm heading out now," I said to the cat.

Satisfied that she'd had enough tap water, Rhonda's cat jumped down and strolled into the living room to catch some sunbeams. She seemed to be even more comfortable in the house than I was. For the past week, I'd kept getting the feeling I wasn't supposed to be there. It had to be the fact that Nisha was away.

As I grabbed my keys to leave the house, I realized that I'd never actually lived by myself before. I'd moved out of my parents' house and straight in with Nisha. Then I'd moved myself into Dalton's house. I'd assumed that, since his place was so spacious and he was frequently at work all day, being there was basically like living alone. I had been lonely a lot. But I hadn't been living on my own. Bernard was always around, plus Dalton did return every night. I'd never truly been alone. Not until now.

And how long had I lasted?

Not very long at all.

After Josie left on Tuesday, I had barely lasted forty-eight hours on my own before I'd adopted Rhonda's cat.

I ran back over to Rhonda's cat, explained how long I expected to be away from the house, and kissed her goodbye.

* * *

Twenty minutes later, I pulled Noah's Mercedes up to a restaurant in an unfamiliar neighborhood.

I waited five minutes for the valet parking attendant to come for my keys when I realized I was back home, not in LA, where valet parking was the norm at the places I went to with Dalton.

Laughing at myself for becoming so spoiled, I rounded the block and squeezed into a parking spot all by myself.

I walked into the restaurant and scanned the dining room for a familiar face.

Adrian Stromquist was there, exactly as I'd planned. He was sitting at a table for six—also as I'd planned—reading something on his phone.

He looked older, somehow, as though the last five months had changed him on the outside as much as I'd changed on the inside. It must have been a trick of the light, or the deepness of his tan. He'd been working in new construction, supervising renovation jobs for wealthy homeowners.

I took a seat across from him without announcing myself.

After a moment, he looked up, startled. "You!" He looked around, eyes wide and hands on the armrests of his chair, as though desperate for an escape route.

"Settle down and don't yell," I said, noting to myself how much I sounded like a kidnapper.

"You've avoided me long enough, Adrian Stromquist. This dinner is happening. I have several of my agents guarding the exits. You're trapped."

He narrowed his eyes. "What?"

"Just kidding about the agents at the exits," I said. "I came alone." I waved the waiter over and told him, "You can pull away this extra table. The other people who were supposed to be coming tonight can't make it. Something came up, and... well, it turns out they weren't actually invited in the first place because they don't exist."

The waiter gave me a disinterested nod and pulled the extra table away.

Adrian stared at me. "Peaches, you can't do this. You have to go. I'm meeting some important potential clients tonight. They need someone to supervise their renovation and installation of..." He trailed off. A scowl spread across his face. Bitterly, he said, "The installation of a heated swimming pool shaped like a peach." He shook his head. "I should have known something was off about those emails."

"You can't blame me for doing what I had to do," I said. "It was the only way I could get you face to face."

He frowned. "But I'm supposed to be meeting twin men and their identical twin wives."

I'd gotten creative with my fake clients. They say it's easier for smart people to swallow a bolder lie. Adrian was always bragging about his near-genius IQ, so I'd leaned hard into the size of my fake story.

Adrian's expression bordered on pouting. "I was looking forward to meeting twins who'd married twins."

"And someday I'm sure you will," I said. "Now, should we order some wine to go with our appetizers? I'm planning to wait until the dessert course to break up. No point in ruining a perfectly good meal." I glanced around. "This place seems appropriate for such an activity."

Adrian said nothing.

The restaurant I'd chosen was across town from where we normally hung out. I'd chosen the location because it wouldn't come preloaded with any old baggage or witnesses who knew us. I fully expected there would be some sort of scene-causing drama from Adrian. He'd raise his voice, eyes flashing with anger, and insult me until I caved and admitted I was unworthy of him. Or something along those lines.

The waiter came by, and I ordered three courses for both of us.

"My treat," I explained. "Plus I know what you like."

Adrian didn't say a word.

We sipped our wine quietly.

When the appetizers came, Adrian said, "These mozzarella sticks aren't bad, but they need dipping sauce."

I got up, grabbed a bottle of ketchup from the waitress station, and squeezed some onto Adrian's plate.

He dipped and ate half of the mozza sticks before he stopped, looked across the table at me, and said softly, "How am I supposed to live without you?"

I was surprised by the earnestness of his question, but I did manage to respond quickly. "You've been fine on your own the last five months."

He stared at me steadily with his icy-blue eyes. "But I haven't been fine," he said, even more softly than before. "Not at all."

I looked down at my plate. My appetite had completely disappeared. I'd expected Angry Adrian, or at the very least, Moody Brooding Adrian. But this was something else. This was Human, Vulnerable Adrian.

My world tilted on its axis.

Everything I'd been expecting to happen at this dinner went away. I was in a scene without a script. I had no idea what was coming next.

He was watching me, waiting for something.

I looked down, avoiding his eyes.

My brain kept recalibrating. All this time, I'd assumed Adrian had been evading my calls and avoiding an official breakup to get under my skin. To get back at me. To mess with my happiness.

I'd never considered that he might have been doing it out of desperation to keep me in his life.

I looked up again. I looked across the table at the handsome, intelligent, funny, flawed man who would always have a piece of my heart, no matter what.

I looked into his eyes and said, "I'm sorry I left without saying goodbye."

He nodded slowly.

The waiter came by and refilled our wine glasses.

Adrian said, "I shouldn't have let you think I was going to propose on New Year's Eve. I've been over it a thousand times in my head, and I can't believe how stupid I was." He leaned forward. "Peaches, I regret every single stupid thing I ever did or said. I regret every time I corrected you on some inconsequential fact. I regret every time I complained about those sticky cough drops you leave everywhere." He clenched his jaw. "Peaches, I missed you." He reached for my hand across the table and grasped my fingers. "I love you."

The waiter arrived with our main course. I yanked my hand away.

"This looks nice," I said of the food.

After the waiter left, Adrian said, "Tell me you don't feel the same way."

The scent of the food in front of me was strong, yet it didn't smell like food. It was steaming my face, making my eyes itch.

He asked, "What's going on with you? How are you feeling about... us?"

I leaned back from the steaming food and turned my head from left to right, avoiding eye contact. "I, uh, have a lot going on right now in my life," I said.

"Such as?"

"It's complicated," I said. "But you have to know that I never meant to hurt you."

He replied, with a sharpness to his voice, "Are you sure about that?"

I jerked my head up, surprised. "What?" I clutched my hand to my chest. "You think I wanted to hurt you?"

He blinked. "They say if you want to understand someone's motivations, you just have to look at the results of their actions."

"Oh, Adrian," I said, feeling myself crumpling before him. "I can't hurt you, and not just because I don't want to. Hurting you is not possible. You're so big, and strong, and smarter than me. You're just so... *Adrian*."

He suddenly pushed his chair back and stood.

"Message received," he said. "Let's make it official." He paused. "It's over."

I mouthed the words he'd spoken. *It's over.*

He repeated them. "It's *officially* over. We're done."

Then he left.

Chapter 30

Saturday, June 3rd

(The Day of Megan's Wedding)

I was happy to have Megan's wedding and my bridesmaid duties to keep my mind occupied.

If I sat still for too long, I tended to think about how sad Adrian had been over dinner.

For the first time ever, I'd seen for myself that big, tough, sarcastic Adrian was a human underneath it all. He could be hurt—*had been hurt*—by me.

I felt awful about it, but also a little angry. I hadn't been perfect, but he was just as much to blame, with all the many, many things he used to do just to irritate me. If there was any blame to go around, it ought to have been shared equally. Fifty fifty.

Then again, was it really anyone's fault when a relationship didn't work out? Dating was supposed to be a trial run, anyway. We'd only been dating, and for less than a year. Sure, the two of us had a long and complicated history, but it wasn't as though we'd committed to more. It wasn't as though we had taken vows, raised a family, and then one of us had betrayed the other during a midlife crisis.

Regardless of who was or wasn't at fault, it didn't do me any good to dwell on it. Thinking it over only made me sweaty, and I'd been instructed not to sweat in my fresh-from-the-dry-cleaners bridesmaid dress.

That Saturday morning, the girls from the wedding party were all at the house—Nisha's house —getting prepared.

I checked on the bride, who was in my bedroom, fussing over her hemline with the seamstress, then went to check on my new cat, who was taking the invasion of her house quite well, considering.

I had just taken a seat on the couch when another bridesmaid, Megan's sister, Tina, came in.

She clutched her swollen belly with one hand while she carefully lowered herself onto a chair across from me. Then she moaned and rubbed her stomach.

"That looks uncomfortable," I said.

She snorted. "You think?"

"What a difference a year makes," I said. "Can you believe it was only a year ago that we were doing this for your wedding?"

Tina frowned. "I barely got to enjoy being a newlywed. Now I'm double pregnant."

Tina wasn't experiencing true double pregnancy —a medical marvel that was rare but did happen. But she was expecting twins, which was a lot for her small frame. Everyone in the family enjoyed teasing her about Luca getting her "double pregnant." He was a big, alpha type of guy, so it made perfect sense to everyone that a guy like that wouldn't stop at one baby. Not that conception worked that way at all... but we liked the idea of it. Luca was a legend.

Both Tina and I were already in our sparkly bridesmaid dresses. Tina's long, dark curls were half up and half in ringlets. My blonde hair was in a similar style. My mother, who would be participating by reading a poem later at the reception, had gone with me to the hair stylist that morning and gotten her hair done exactly the same.

Tina moaned again. "This wedding had better not start late," she said. "I feel like a beached whale with flipper feet already, and my feet are only going to get more swollen through the day."

"You may be a whale, but you're a gorgeous whale," I said. "I'd tell you that you look *radiant*, but I don't want to get punched."

"I'm more of a wrestler than a puncher." She grinned. "But not in this condition." She winced and shifted in her chair as she spoke down to her belly. "Calm down, you two."

"Are they active today?"

"*Active* is an understatement. These two tumbleweeds are definitely up to something." She wiped her brow with the back of her hand.

I asked, "Do you think today could be the day? With all the excitement and everything? I know you're not due for a few more days, but everyone knows babies don't have calendars in there."

"They do not," she said. "Just between us, I've been talking to them, telling them they can come out a little early. I mean, not this instant. If I *were* to feel any sort of contractions, I'd be able to hold them in for a few more hours." She bit her lower lip. "That's a thing, right?"

"I don't believe that's a thing," I said. "I don't think you have any say in it once things start rolling. And you do look ready to pop."

She gave me an alarmed look. "What if I'm standing up there during the ceremony, and they suddenly start shooting out of me in front of everyone?"

"Don't you worry about a thing," I said calmly. "I've already discussed it with your sister. You're in good hands with me. I'll catch those babies like a pro. You might even start a new family tradition. Catching the babies instead of the bouquet."

Tina stared at me blankly. "I may be at the stage of pregnancy where I cannot appreciate your sense of humor."

"That's not going to stop me," I said.

She leaned back and put her feet up on a floral ottoman. "What a crazy year it's been." She glanced around the living room, her gaze settling on Rhonda's cat, who was snoozing on top of her new carpet-covered cat tree.

Tina cocked her head up at Rhonda's cat and spoke sweetly. "Hello, you gorgeous thing! Where did you come from? Oh my goodness, look at your little white paws!" Tina and her sister both adored their cat, Muffins. They used to dress the orange tabby in baby clothes for photos.

"This is Rhonda's cat," I said proudly. "Well, she's mine now. I'm a cat mama."

"Being a cat mama suits you," Tina said. "You look really good, by the way. Is it because you and Adrian are back together?"

"What?"

She covered her mouth with her hand. "I'm sorry. I just assumed... since your actor fellow isn't around..." She wrinkled her nose. "What happened? Are you not back with Adrian?"

"Adrian and I officially broke up last night. It was over dinner. In person. Face to face." I knew I was being redundant but I went on, to be clear. "I got verbal confirmation in front of witnesses, assuming anyone around us was paying attention. Adrian Stromquist and I are completely over."

"Except you both still... *you know*." We were alone in the living room, but she didn't spill my secret about Elliot. She'd been told all about it by Megan, with my family's permission.

"That will always connect us," I said, feeling very grownup for a change. "But it wasn't enough. Back in high school, I used to fantasize that Adrian and I were soul mates."

"A person can have more than one soul mate," Tina said, her eyes glistening. "There's more than one other soul who can fit with yours perfectly."

I laughed out loud at the idea that Adrian had been anything near perfect.

She asked, "Are you sure it's over?"

"Here's the thing," I said. "I'd probably still be wondering about me and Adrian if dating him had been the road not taken. But I *did* take that road. We were together long enough for me to get a real taste of what life with him would be like. To his credit, it was never dull. He did enjoy pushing my buttons, but I got a kick out of pushing his, too." I got up and went over to the cat tree so I could pet Rhonda's cat while I talked. "If I'd left Adrian for Dalton, I might have questioned my decision, but now that Dalton's not really in the picture, and I still don't want to be with Adrian, I can be sure."

Rhonda's cat lifted her head for chin scratches. Her white moustache curled up in a grin.

When I turned around again, Tina's expression caught me by surprise. She was pale and grimacing.

Through gritted teeth, she said, "What do you mean Dalton's not in the picture? Does that mean you two are over?"

"Not officially, but I'm sure it's coming," I said, my heart sinking as I acknowledged the sad reality. "He's dead-set against my career, and I can't be with someone who doesn't support my dreams, no matter how rich or handsome or talented he is. I'm too young to settle for a life of charity lunches with hyena ladies."

Tina breathed in and out rapidly. Her pale face turned red. "That's... I'm sorry to hear it. I guess you'll be sticking around here..." She huffed and puffed.

"Tina, you are in labor," I said.

"No, I'm not," she said.

"You're sweating like a sinner in church," I said, moving toward her.

She raised a hand, waving for me to stay back. "It's okay. I can hold them in for a few more hours. They've been in there nine months. What's the rush?"

"How far apart are the contractions?"

She winced. "They started this morning, and they weren't bad, so I haven't been timing them." She let out a big breath. "I'm fine." She frowned. "Oh, no!" There was more huffing and puffing.

"Is that the same one, or a new one?"

She gave me a helpless look. "Meenie's going to kill me! She already lost one bridesmaid, and now she's going to kill meeeee!" The last part came out as a scream.

Megan's seamstress, who had been in my bedroom with Megan, came running into the living room to see what the screaming was about.

The seamstress saw the state that Tina was in and dropped her pincushion.

Rhonda's cat jumped off her carpeted perch and immediately smacked the red, tomato-shaped pincushion under the sofa.

Both Tina and the seamstress started panicking together, hyperventilating and looking to me for guidance. The cat dove under the couch and began chasing the tomato around the room.

Tina wailed, "Peaches, do something!"

How would I know what to do? I felt like I was on stage for an expectant audience, and all out of material.

Suddenly, an idea came to me. It came from wherever it was all great ideas came from. A wave of calm washed over me, and a smile crossed my lips. I felt a lot like I did whenever I came up with the perfect comeback to a heckler.

In a reassuring tone, I said to Tina, "Megan won't kill you. Not if we act fast." I went to her side. "First of all, get this dress off before you get twin juice on it."

Tina shot me a dirty look.

"Take it off so *someone else* can wear the dress," I said.

The seamstress said, "But who?"

I asked her, "What size is the bust on Tina's dress?"

Tina made an indignant sound, but the seamstress gave me the answer.

"That's my size," I said.

Then I explained my plan to the seamstress.

"That might work," she said, then she ran off to run interception with Megan.

Tina got her phone and called her husband. "It's happening," she said glumly. I heard his loud whoop on the other end of the line.

I snuck into my bedroom, grabbed some clothes for Tina to wear to the hospital, and then got her changed out of the dress while we waited for Luca to arrive. He would be there in a few minutes to take her straight to the hospital for the birth.

He arrived, beaming and red-faced, and I immediately made him strip off his tuxedo. The suit would be a little large for the groomsman I had in mind, but too big was better than too small.

I loaned Luca a pair of gray sweatpants and a zip-up hoodie. It was from a women's line of clothing, but Luca was so manly that it looked perfect on him, albeit a bit short in the leg.

Thirty minutes later, before Megan had even discovered that her sister had gone missing, a new plan was in place.

All thanks to me.

Peaches Monroe saves the day!

Chapter 31

Except for the part where a bridesmaid had to bail to give birth to twins, the wedding went perfectly.

The minister hit the perfect tone for the couple, the right people cried at the right time, and nobody fainted, vomited, or gave birth on the altar.

At the end of the ceremony, as we prepared to head outside for photos, my mother squeezed my arm and said, "Thank you so much." She had been standing next to me the whole time, wearing the dress that had been meant for Tina.

I said, "Thank *you* for agreeing to fill in for Tina. Megan talks tough, but she would have been devastated if she'd lost another bridesmaid."

She giggled. "Imagine that. Me, a bridesmaid, at my age." She leaned in and whispered, "Your father can't take his eyes off me."

I looked over at my father, who seemed to be on the verge of crying. Again.

He was wearing Luca's suit, which fit him well enough. The pants had been way too long, but the seamstress had tucked them up in a jiffy.

I put my arm around my mother and posed for a picture as the photographer came by.

The photographer commented on how perfectly the modified dress fit my mother, and how much the two of us looked alike. We could have been twins, or at least sisters.

My mother giggled and blushed at the flattery.

We headed outside and posed for more pictures.

"Your cousins both made such lovely brides," my mother commented as she watched Megan pose. "However, I'm not sure about some of the language in Megan's vow. Didn't you think it was a bit... odd? All that talk about... was it costumes?"

"Megan wrote her vows herself," I said.

"That explains a lot," my mother said. Everyone knew Megan was a bit odd.

Just then, everyone's phones began buzzing at once.

We all pulled out our phones and read the group text message from Luca.

My father read it out loud, "A healthy baby girl and a healthy baby boy. The mother is resting and recovering from delivery!"

Everyone cheered for Tina, Luca, and their twins.

My mother said to me, "It's too bad your Dalton couldn't make it to this one. Have you heard from him about how his pitch meeting went?"

"I'm sure he'll be in touch when it fits his schedule," I said.

My mother took both of my hands and stared into my eyes. "Peaches, I have to tell you something."

"What? Why are you holding my hands?" I pretended to pull away. "I don't want to catch your menopause, woman."

She shook her head but didn't break eye contact.

I stopped joking and asked what it was she had to tell me.

"Never mind," she said.

"No," I said. "Say it."

She smiled and released my hands. "Forget I said anything. I'm going to check on your father. You'd better go see if Megan needs anything."

Then she walked away.

I stood on the grassy lawn in front of the church, wondering what she'd been about to tell me.

I watched as my mother joined a small group of people who were hugging and shaking hands.

To my left, a dark car with tinted windows rolled by slowly and then parked up the street.

The car doors opened, and two men stepped out.

One was Dalton Deangelo, and the other was his trainer friend, Tyler. They were far away, but I'd know those two anywhere.

My heart began to beat rapidly. He'd made it after all! Not to the ceremony, but he'd be there for the party, which was also important.

I swallowed hard and tried to calm myself.

Dalton had flown or driven up for the wedding, even though I'd told him not to bother. He'd ignored me, which was actually a good thing.

Why had I told him not to come up, anyway? It was the exact opposite of what I truly wanted. I wasn't one of those girls who sabotaged perfectly good relationships, and yet I'd all but assumed we were breaking up... over what?

Over his uncomfortable yet polite reaction to my comedy routine, in which I'd made fun of him for several minutes?

Suddenly, his reaction to my act didn't seem like such a crime.

And then, when he'd wanted to make his pitch meeting a priority, what had I done? Had I shown his career the level of support that I'd demanded for mine? No. I had not. I'd actually behaved rather selfishly. For good reason, of course, but... still selfishly.

But now he was there. In the flesh. Back to where the magic had started happening a year ago.

My whole body vibrated with excitement as I felt the love I had for Dalton welling up inside me. I couldn't wait to tell him how sorry I was, and how the only thing that mattered was that the two of us were together, and I wasn't going to let any more of my dumb ideas or knee-jerk reactions keep us apart.

He was there, and he was mine. I pulsed with joy just watching him from afar.

I watched as Dalton Deangelo, the love of my life, walked up behind a woman in a bridesmaid dress.

That bridesmaid had her blond hair styled the same as mine.

That woman was my mother.

I watched from twenty feet away as Dalton tapped my mother on the shoulder, waited until she whirled around, and grabbed her for a huge, passionate kiss.

There was a surprised murmur as the rest of the wedding party noticed the same thing.

Everyone stared. The photographer took pictures.

Dalton dipped my mother and continued holding her in his embrace. People whistled. My father stood by, too shocked to move.

And my mother... she didn't seem to be trying very hard to alert Dalton to his error.

I had to admit, from where I stood, his embrace did look awfully romantic.

I glanced over at Tyler, who made eye contact with me. His jaw dropped. Then the personal trainer jumped into action, quickly separating Dalton from my mother. My mother straightened up and began staggering in confused circles, one hand held to her cheek.

The whole wedding party erupted in chaos.

Tyler pointed Dalton toward the real Peaches, and my guy came running toward me.

"Your mother," he said, gasping.

"Enough about my mother," I said, and I kissed him as the whole wedding party cheered.

Chapter 32

Sunday, June 4th

(The Day after the Wedding)

Dalton pulled the T-shirt I'd just thrown into the cardboard box out again.

"You can't throw this one away," he said.

We were in my old bedroom, and he was helping me pack up my belongings to make space for Noah's stuff. Noah would be setting up a recording studio in my old room after he and Nisha returned from their honeymoon travels.

It was noon, and Dalton and I had planned to get an early start on packing, but we'd only just started. Time had gotten away from us. Dalton and I had been separated for a full week, and we'd had a lot to catch up on. We'd even talked a bit.

"I'm not throwing that shirt away," I said. "That's the donation box. The shirt will go on to another good home."

Dalton sniffed the shirt. "I love this shirt."

"You've never seen that shirt."

"That's not true. You were wearing this the first time I saw you at the donut shop."

I rolled my eyes. "You are so sentimental! You sound like Noah. He gets all weird and emotional about Nisha's clothing."

"I am not weird and emotional!" He pretended to be offended. "It's a good shirt. I like how it fits."

"There are moth holes in the armpits," I said. "If we haul that back with us, Bernard is going to have a conniption on laundry day."

"I have lots of shirts with holes," Dalton said.

"Bernard will know it's an old shirt and not a fake-old designer shirt. They always put the fake moth holes somewhere visible, not in the armpits."

"You let me deal with Bernard," Dalton said, and he tossed the shirt into the keeper box.

A second later, a black-and-white cat shot out of the box, wearing the shirt like a cape until it fell off. Rhonda's cat gave us a dirty look for disturbing her midday nap before padding off to see what Tyler was up to in the living room. She enjoyed jumping on his back and going for a ride while he did his hundred pushups.

I called after her, "Behave yourself, Rhonda's cat!" I turned back to Dalton and said, "We need to come up with a better name for that cat."

"How about Muffins?"

"She's black and white. Muffins is the name for an orange cat. And besides, there's already a Muffins in the family. Megan's cat's name is Muffins."

"How about Bernice? We can pretend she's our other butler."

"Bernard would be so jealous. You know how it is with sibling rivalry."

Dalton snickered. "How about Fanny?"

"Now you're just being ridiculous."

"Aren't cat names supposed to be ridiculous?"

"I don't know," I said, then I pulled out my comedy notebook and made a note to explore that concept more. People enjoyed pet-based humor. It wasn't the freshest subject matter, but it was relatable.

Dalton stood up on his tiptoes and tried to get a peek at my notebook.

I snapped it shut and put it away quickly. "Not until it's more thought out," I said.

"I heard you in the shower, talking about how I kissed your mom at the wedding. You really think that's funny?"

"It's literally the funniest thing that has ever happened in our entire family, going back ten generations," I said.

"I guess it was kind of funny," he said. "I felt bad at the time."

"That's why it's funny. Tragedy plus time equals comedy."

"Oh," he said, and continued folding clothes.

After a minute, Dalton said, "You can stay up here a bit longer, if you'd like. I do have to be back Monday morning for shooting, but you can take all the time you need. I can have BB change the date on your plane ticket no problem."

"I want to be wherever you are," I said.

"But this is... your home." He looked around my room. We'd already taken down my artwork. The walls were bare and in need of a coat of paint, but the room was still cozy.

"*You're* my home," I said.

He nodded, crossed by me, and yelled from the doorway. "Hey, Tyler! I got the line. She should say, 'You're my home!' It gets the point across without being too much on the nose!"

I must have supplied a much-needed line of dialog for their screenplay, which now had a romance subplot.

I gave Dalton a dead-eyed look. "Way to ruin a moment, dude."

He smiled, gave me a quick kiss, and said, "I'm sure we'll have plenty more moments."

"I want a writing credit for my efforts."

"I'll thank you when I accept my Oscar."

I poked him in the ribs. "I ain't waitin' that long!"

"Hey, now," he said, backing away carefully and putting the bed between us. "We have an agreement. I can use the crazy stuff you come up with in my screenplay, and you can tell funny stories about me in your act. Fair is fair."

"Fine," I said, since we had agreed on that.

"About that night when you did your bridesmaid material," Dalton said casually. "I didn't run out of the club just because of how it felt to hear myself being talked about like that."

"I know, I know. It's your allergies."

"It wasn't that," he said, looking me in the eyes. "It's because I saw someone there who looked like they wouldn't be able to keep a secret."

I rolled my eyes. "It was me," I said. "I'm the one who can't keep a secret."

"Not that," he said. "It was... someone I dealt with when I was inspecting the club."

"What? Why were you inspecting the club?"

"Because I bought it," he said. "I own the comedy club."

I crossed my arms. "You what? You bought the comedy club just so you could shut down my career? That is... unbelievable."

He crossed his arms the way I had, mocking me. Grinning, he said, "I bought the comedy club so you and your friends could keep performing there. You know the renovations they were always talking about? There were renovations in the works, all right. It was supposed to be getting knocked down by a wrecking ball back in May. After I closed the deal, I ordered actual renovations to keep up the cover story. I didn't want people at the club to know I'd bought it. I own it through a holding company, and nobody should know, as long as we don't tell them."

What he was saying actually checked out. I had heard rumors to that effect, but hadn't wanted to believe it.

I stared at him in shock. Dalton had bought the run-down, dirty old comedy club just so I could keep hanging out there with my new friends? What kind of person did something like that?

Dalton shyly looked away. "I'd been looking for a long-term investment anyway, so I figured why not? I bought the contract from the developer. They made a quick profit without the risk of construction, and I... well, I'm sure it will pay off in the long run. The thing about investments is—"

He didn't get to finish because I'd tackled him, thrown him on the bed, and started covering his face with kisses.

Chapter 33

July

(One Month Later)

Nisha and Noah came to visit us in California on the last leg of their cross-country journey. They planned to stay for two nights then make their way home again. Noah was eager to set up his recording studio. He played classical guitar beautifully, which I hadn't known until that day.

The four of us were gathered in the games room—formerly Dalton's cardboard box room—playing a game of pool on the new pool table.

Noah looked at Dalton and said, "That trailer you got us, man. It's so nice. We couldn't have survived the trip without it. How did you know?" His eyes started to well up. "You're like the brother I never had," he said, and he launched himself at Dalton for the third hug of the day.

Nisha, who was standing beside me, turned to me and said, "Noah's really in touch with his feelings."

I replied, "Don't tell him we only bought the trailer to make you guys feel bad about not inviting us to your wedding."

She wrinkled her nose. "I suspected that might have been your intention. But it really was a great gift. No hard feelings."

I laughed and took a sip of my import beer. "I'm glad you're able to forgive us for the overly generous gift." I looked down at the bottle. "This is really good beer. Here. Have a taste." I thrust the bottle at her lips.

She grimaced and pulled away like I'd been offering her poison. It wasn't like Nisha to refuse a taste or sip of whatever I was enjoying, so I instantly had my theory confirmed.

"You're pregnant," I said, quietly enough so the boys wouldn't overhear.

She smiled shyly and ran her hand over her dark, short hair. "I was going to tell you tonight anyway. I couldn't keep it from you."

"How far along?"

"Just a few months," she said.

"Are you double pregnant or single pregnant?"

"Just single pregnant," she said. "Noah is quite the man, but he's no Luca Lowell."

We both snickered.

I said, "What about Noah's recording studio? That must be off the table now. You'll have to turn my old room into a nursery."

"Maybe not," she said. "Adrian is going to put some insulation in that back room we used for storage. It's got a window, and while it's not huge, it should work for a few years."

I nodded and carefully avoided saying anything about Adrian. My new strategy for hearing him mentioned was to pretend there was a new friend in Nisha and Noah's life, and he just happened to share the same name as the guy I'd once had history with.

"Wow," I said of the nursery plans. "You've thought this whole baby thing through."

She shrugged. "As much as a person can," she said, taking in a big breath. "Life is going to change a lot soon."

"Change can be good," I said.

The guys, who'd been chatting on their own, excused themselves to go check out Dalton's gym. Noah was particularly excited to see the new Pilates equipment.

With the guys gone, Nisha and I lost interest in playing pool by the actual rules, and started making up our own game, in which we rolled the balls around at the same time.

The cat came strolling in and jumped up on the pool table to see what all the noise was about, as well as to provide her disapproval. If it wasn't the butler popping his head in to frown about weird noises, it was the cat.

"Hello there, Rocket," Nisha said, leaning forward to pet the black-and-white feline.

"What did you just call her?"

"Rocket," Nisha said. "That's her name."

"How did you know? The people at Donut Joe's didn't know her name, and neither did anyone at the animal shelter."

"Rhonda told me once," Nisha said. "The cat's name is Rocket. It's short for *Rhonda's cat*. Rhonda sure had a sense of humor, didn't she? I'm going to miss that woman."

"Rocket, short for Rhonda's cat," I repeated.

The cat cocked her head and stared at me intensely.

"Rocket," I said again. The cat's ears twitched in a way I'd never seen them twitch before. It had to be recognition.

Nisha smiled and patted her very small baby bump. "Maybe I'll name the little one Naby, as in short for Nisha and Noah's baby."

I pretended to barf.

Nisha said, "I'm so glad you haven't become one of those fake Hollywood types who only says whatever other people want to hear."

"You're one of the few who appreciate my honesty," I said. "Actually, that's not true. Comedians are brutal. They claim to be brutally honest, but some of them are just plain brutal. They think it's okay if they say something like 'Real talk!' right after insulting you."

"Ouch," Nisha said. "Sounds toxic."

"No way," I said. "I mean, yes, it probably sounds that way from the outside, but if you're part of the group, you know that casual cruelty is how they show their affection."

"As long as you're happy," Nisha said, then, "Are you? Happy?"

"Look around," I said.

"You never cared that much about material things," she said. "I know that all of this could go away overnight and you wouldn't mind."

I clutched at my imaginary pearls. "They can take my jewelry, but they can't take away my butler."

Nisha walked around the pool table and spun two more balls in a spiral arc across the green.

"You seem to be enjoying your life here," she said.

"I am," I agreed. "I might be almost as happy on the inside as you and Noah are on the outside."

"And we're happy through and through," she said. "So, I guess everything worked out in the end. There were a few bumps along the way, but we got there." She started to tear up but fought it back. "Bloody pregnancy hormones," she said, waving her hand in front of her face.

"Tell me about it."

She gasped.

"You're not..."

I laughed so hard. "I'm not, I swear. But I was, once. If you think pregnancy hormones are bad you should try combining them with puberty."

Her expression turned sad, and she looked down at her growing stomach.

"I can't imagine what you must have gone through with Elliot," she said.

"It was tough, but it all worked out in the end," I said.

Just then, Rocket walked through the middle of the pool table and whacked a ball with her paw.

Nisha and I both laughed as the cat sank two balls.

As I wiped the corners of my eyes, I realized that not only was I happy, but I was happier than I'd ever been. I was probably too happy to make it as a comedian—the best ones were notoriously wounded—but that was fine by me.

Thanks to fate, and Dalton Deangelo, and his entire wacky family, I'd gotten to a wonderful place in my life. Perhaps my comedy would suffer, but I wouldn't have wanted it any other way.

With Rocket's help, we finished sinking the pool balls, and then left the games room.

As we walked down the hallway, I said, "Nisha, you know how you always ruin perfectly good books by flipping to the last page and reading it first?"

"Yes," she said hesitantly.

"Like some sort of maniac," I said.

"Yes," she said again, growing annoyed.

"This moment, right now, would be the end of the romance book about you and Noah. This page, with you complaining about pregnancy hormones while talking about how happy you are."

She frowned. "But our story's not over. It's only just getting started."

"I know," I said. "That's what makes it so good when you finally get there. Standing on the precipice of a bright future is the high point. It's like the *closer*, the big laugh-getter that comedians end their act on."

"I can see that," Nisha said. "What about your story? Is this the last page?"

"Oh, my life is too crazy for a book," I said. "Nobody would ever believe it. I mean, come on. A drool-worthy TV actor falls head over heels in love with a regular curvy girl working at a bookstore? Then, at the same time, she also wins the heart of her old high school crush? Then she has to choose between the two gorgeous men who are fighting over her? It's a bit much, don't you think? Plus I stole a car, among other things. People don't like heroines who commit crimes."

"Oh, Peaches," Nisha said. "People would believe it if they knew you like I did, and loved you like I do."

I put my arm around her. "I love you, too. Can I pick the name for the baby?"

Her jaw dropped.

"Peaches!"

"As the baby's godmother, I believe it is within my rights."

She shot me a dirty look.

I told her we had plenty of time to discuss the matter, and we continued down the hallway to find our guys.

The end of Peaches Monroe's Diary Book 4,
Peaches on Top.

Look for other titles by Angie Pepper
for cameos from your favorite Baker Street characters!

www.angelapepper.com